MAHY MAGIC

Books by Margaret Mahy

Picture Books

The Boy Who Was Followed Home *illustrated by Steven Kellogg*
The Witch in the Cherry Tree *illustrated by Jenny Williams*
The Man Whose Mother Was a Pirate *illustrated by Margaret Chamberlain*
A Lion in the Meadow *illustrated by Jenny Williams*
Jam *illustrated by Helen Craig*

Story Collections

The Great Piratical Rumbustification *and* The Librarian and the Robbers
illustrated by Quentin Blake
The Birthday Burglar *and* A Very Wicked Headmistress
illustrated by Margaret Chamberlain
The Chewing-Gum Rescue and Other Stories *illustrated by Jan Ormerod*
A Lion in the Meadow and Five Other Favourites
illustrated with black and white drawings
Leaf Magic and Five Other Favourites *illustrated by Margaret Chamberlain*
The Third Margaret Mahy Story Book *illustrated by Shirley Hughes*
The Downhill Crocodile Whizz and Other Stories *illustrated by Ian Newsham*

Novels

The Tricksters
The Changeover *A Supernatural Romance*
WINNER OF THE CARNEGIE MEDAL 1984
The Haunting
WINNER OF THE CARNEGIE MEDAL 1982
The Pirates' Mixed-Up Voyage *illustrated by Margaret Chamberlain*
Raging Robots and Unruly Uncles *illustrated by Peter Stevenson*

Margaret Mahy

MAHY MAGIC

A collection of
the most magical stories from the
Margaret Mahy Story Books

Illustrated by Shirley Hughes

J.M. Dent & Sons Limited
London & Melbourne

First published in 1986
Printed in Great Britain
at Mackays Ltd, Chatham
for J.M. Dent & Sons Ltd
33 Welbeck Street, London W1M 8LX

From **The First Margaret Mahy Story Book**
Teddy and the Witches, Right-Hand Men, The Road to
School, The Thief and the Magic, The Great Tractor
Rescue, Green Needles, The Witch Dog

From **The Second Margaret Mahy Story Book**
The Merry-Go-Round, the Bird Child, Kite Saturday,
The Good Wizard of the Forest, The Kings of the Broom
Cupboard

From **The Third Margaret Mahy Story Book**
Aunt Nasty, Looking for a Ghost, The Witch Doctor,
The Boy Who Bounced, The Princess and the Clown,
The Green Fair

Cataloguing in Publication Data

Mahy Margaret
    Mahy magic: a collection of the most
    magical stories from Margaret Mahy Story books.
    I. Title
    823 (J)   PZ7

ISBN 0-460-06184-4

Contents

Teddy and the Witches

Once there were three witches flying over the world and looking down at it from their broomsticks. One had white hair, one had black hair, and one had hair like wild bright flame, and all three had gleaming golden eyes. . . . They were looking for mischief to do.

At last they came to a long, green valley which they had never seen before in all their magic lives, and their eyes shone as they looked at the snug-as-a-bug-in-a-rug farms and the soft, smudgy shadows in the creases of the hills.

"Here," they said to each other, "is a wonderful place for some mischief." And they smiled. . . .

The first witch pointed her finger. *Tweedle dee!* All the pigs grew silver wings and flew up into the trees with the magpies.

The second witch clapped her hands and all the hens turned into parrots and cockatoos—scarlet and green, white and yellow—and filled the air with their merry screechings.

But the third witch, the red-headed one, just blinked her golden eyes and all the cows became elephants—and elephants eat a lot of grass and are very hard to milk.

1

Then the witches sat back to enjoy the mischief, like wasps round a honey pot.

Now, in this valley lived a small boy called Teddy. He had brown eyes, he was always hungry, and his head was full of deep, secret ways of thinking. And when he went out the next morning and found the hen run full of parrots and cockatoos he thought to himself, "Witches!" And when he saw Next-Door-Farmer's fields full of large grey crumpled-looking elephants he thought to himself, "Witches!" And then when he heard the pigs squealing in the trees, he thought, "It's those witches again. I must do something about them."

And so Teddy sat down with a ball of string and some

2

ends of rope and worked at a secret thing. His mother walked by him to the clothesline

"What are you making, little Teddy?" she asked. "Is it a net of some kind?"

"It isn't a net," Teddy answered. "It's called 'Little Hand Snatching at the Stars'."

His mother smiled and went on her way. She did not know that "Little Hand Snatching at the Stars" was part of a witch trap.

It was late in the afternoon when the witch trap was finished. Teddy hung it between two tall pine trees, and on the ground underneath the trap he put some pieces of a broken mirror, two shining tin lids and some teaspoons which he had taken from the drawer when his mother wasn't looking. The idea was that the witches would see these bright things shining and would fly down to see what they were. And then they would be caught in the trap. . . .

Sure enough, next morning when Teddy looked out of the window, he saw something like a flame caught beneath the pine trees. There, very beautiful and glowing, was the youngest witch—the red-headed one—like a fly in a spider's web. Down on the ground lay her pointed hat, her cloak and broomstick.

Teddy ran out into the garden.

"Hello little fellow," she said very sweetly to Teddy. "Could you pass me my broomstick and hat please?"

Teddy knew that a witch's magic lies in her hat and broomstick. He did not give them to her, but took them inside and hid them in his wardrobe behind the raincoats. Then he took a skipping-rope, and went out to the witch again. After he had set her free from the witch trap, Teddy tied the skipping-rope round her ankles.

"What are you going to do with me?" she asked, so

3

sweetly that it was hard to believe she would do any mischief. But in the next paddock Teddy could see great bare patches eaten by elephants that had once been cows.

"During the day," he said, "you will be able to help my mother. But at night I will tie you up to the hen house. If it rains you can get inside." (This was not at all cruel as witches are used to perching at night.)

"But I don't like parrots," said the witch, looking at the gaily-coloured hen run.

"You should have thought of that before," Teddy answered.

"Well, I won't be here long anyway," said the witch, with a toss of her wild red hair. "My sisters will set me free very quickly and you will be sorry you ever thought of making a witch trap."

Teddy's mother was surprised when he brought the witch inside, but she listened to his story and said that the witch might dry the breakfast dishes. At first the witch was sulky and cross, but as the morning passed she grew more cheerful. Then, just before lunch, the grocer's van drove up and the young driver got out to bring in the box of groceries that Teddy's mother had ordered.

It was plain the witch was very pleased with his black curly hair and merry eyes.

"Is he a prince?" she asked Teddy.

"No, he's the grocer's man," Teddy answered.

"How are you, fellow," the grocer's man said to Teddy as he came in. He looked at the witch. It was plain he was very pleased with her wild red hair and golden eyes. After he had talked for a while he went off—leaving a dozen eggs that should have gone to somebody else. After this the witch seemed almost happy.

Before he went to bed that night Teddy pinned a spray of fern to his pyjamas. He had read somewhere that it was a good protection against witch spells. It was just as well he did, for in the night there was more witch trouble. . . .

5

Teddy had fallen asleep when, suddenly, his bed shook itself and then flew out of the window. Outside, the two witches screamed at him.

"Give us back our sister," they screeched. They flew at him, making claws with their long fingers. "Give us back our sister or you will go for a wild ride."

Teddy was not afraid. He answered, "First you must take the magic off the valley and give us back our cows and hens."

"Never, never!" yelled the witches. They tried to magic Teddy, but the spells bounced back with a twanging sound. This was because of the fern Teddy was wearing.

"Well," said the white-haired witch, "we may not be able to touch you, but we can change your bed."

Then Teddy's bed began to buck and kick, to slide and glide, to bumble and stumble, to creep and leap, and to highstep and lowstep, until Teddy felt quite giddy.

"Will you set her free?" the witches screamed. (They could not rescue her themselves without her broomstick and hat and cloak, and of course they did not know where Teddy had hidden them.)

"Of course I won't," Teddy answered.

Then his bed became a wild horse, with furious wings and hoofs of thunder, and it raced wildly up and down the valley. But Teddy held on tightly with his knees, and twisted his hands in its mane—and after a while the horse stood still.

Then the bed became a fiery dragon which hissed and twisted to get at Teddy, but he curled up small between the dragon's wings, and it could not get him. And so, in its turn, the dragon grew still.

And then the bed became a great wind and it tossed Teddy like thistledown, but he lay limp in the wind and

6

thought happy thoughts, and pretended he was being bounced in his bed at home.

At last the white-haired witch said, "That was just my sister's magic. I'm going to send you round the world!" She said something to the bed which at once set off at a terrific speed and flew all the way round the world. But Teddy sat in the middle of his bed and sang nursery rhymes and took no notice at all of the hot or the cold, or the green or the gold, or the pounding, bounding sea. At last the bed came home again, and as it did so, there was the sound of breaking violin strings. The witches had taken their spells off the valley. Down from the trees floated the pigs. The silver wings shook themselves free and fluttered

7

off to another place. Where they went I can't tell you at all. And the parrots and cockatoos—scarlet and green, white and yellow—became clucking, scratching hens again.

Then the oldest witch—the white-haired one—said to Teddy, "The mischief is undone, as far as we can undo it. Our sister must undo her own spell, and turn the elephants back to cows." Then they flew away into the new morning that was poking its bright face over the hills.

When he got up, Teddy went into the kitchen. The witch was putting apples on the stove to stew for breakfast.

She wore one of his mother's aprons, and her long red hair hung in a pigtail down her back.

"Your sisters have taken off their magic," Teddy told her. "And if you turn the elephants back to cows I will give you back your broomstick, cloak and hat."

"My sisters?" said the witch. "My broomstick? Oh yes, that's right. I'm a witch! I had forgotten." She waved her hand and there was the sound of a bell note, faint, far away and rather sad. "There now, the magic is gone."

"Well, thank you," Teddy answered. "I'll go and get your broomstick."

"Keep it yourself," said the witch. "I don't want it. I like it here. I'm tired of being a witch. Besides, tonight I'm going to the pictures with the grocer's man."

"Really, I can't think what I'd do without her," said Teddy's mother. "She is such a help to me. It's just like magic."

The witch looked pleased.

Teddy thought for a while. "Can I really have your hat and broomstick?" he asked, at last.

"You might as well," she answered, "for I don't want them."

The people in the valley had just got over their surprise at finding their pigs, hens and cows had come back to them, when they were surprised again to see Teddy on a broomstick and wearing a high steeple hat, flying overhead.

"There's that Teddy!" they said to each other. "What will he be up to next?"

The broomstick flicked a bit as if it were laughing. But Teddy pointed upwards, and it flew higher and higher, like a little bird trying to reach the sun. Up into the blue, blue air it went, and there Teddy soared and swooped like a small wind, happy among the clouds.

9

The Boy who Bounced

Once there was a little boy who had a very bad habit indeed. He used to bounce like a ball. Wherever he went his mother would say:

"Walk like a little gentleman." But he wouldn't. He bounced instead. His father said:

"No one in our family has ever bounced before. I wish you would do something else. You could run a bit, or even hop, or you could skip."

The little boy took no notice at all. This was a mistake because one day he bounced on a magician who was snoozing in the sun. The magician was very cross.

"It is really too much," he cried. "I came out for a quiet day in the country and what happens? First I'm chased by a bull (I had to turn it into a canary bird to get away). Then I'm chased by the farmer who owned the bull (I had to change a foxglove into a lot of money to pay him). It has left me very tired. I lie down to have a snooze and a nasty little boy comes and bounces on me. Pah! Say you're sorry, little boy, and walk off quietly."

The rude little boy took no notice of the magician. He started to bounce away. The magician became very angry indeed.

"If you want to bounce, well, bounce you shall," he declared, and began to mutter magic words very quickly. The little boy felt suddenly strange about the fingers and toes—a sort of pins and needles feeling. (That was the magic working.) Before he could say "Mousetrap!" he had turned into a red rubber ball— a big ball, a bouncing ball. He could bounce so softly that he wouldn't break a cobweb if he bounced on it. He could bounce as high as a pine tree.

"Meet me here in a year's time," the magician said, "and I'll think about whether or not to turn you into a boy again." Then he lay down and began to snooze once more.

The Bouncer leaped over the creek and began to go round the world. He felt quite happy because now he could bounce so much better than before. As he went past the school all the children came running out trying to catch him, but he went too fast for them. Soon he reached the sea.

He couldn't bounce very easily on the water.

11

Instead the waves helped him along. They were delighted to have such a fine red ball to play with and they tossed him to one another until he reached Africa.

Lions opened their yellow eyes as the Bouncer went past and the giraffes stretched their necks to see him. They stretched them so far that all the giraffes in that part of Africa have longer necks than any other giraffes which makes them very proud and conceited.

He went through all sorts of countries with names I can't spell, and his fine red paint wore off so he became a grey battered-looking bouncer. He went more

slowly now and had to stop to catch his breath. When he stopped, he hid. It was one day while he was hiding that he overheard two men talking.

"I hear they have caught a wicked magician," the first man said.

"Well, I don't know if he is wicked or not," the second man said in reply, "but they are going to beat him. Would you like to come and watch?"

"Yes I would," said the first man.

"How unfair!" the Bouncer thought. "Poor magician! I shall rescue him!" He followed the men, bouncing so softly they did not hear him.

The magician was brought out from prison, and twelve men in black stood with sticks to beat him. He looked small and old and his gingery whiskers drooped sadly. "That isn't my magician," the Bouncer thought, "but he is very like him."

Then, just as the twelve men were lifting their sticks to beat the magician, the Bouncer gave a tremendous *bounce* and knocked them all head over heels. Quick as a cat the magician leaped onto the Bouncer's back and off they went on great high bounces as high as the trees.

"Turn to the left," the magician whispered. "Then go over the river and turn to the right. We will be in another country after that and we will find my brother snoozing beside a creek."

So the Bouncer did as he was told and, sure enough, it wasn't long before he recognized his home and the creek where he had bounced on the first magician. There the first magician was—still snoozing, with grass growing over him, looking like an old mossy log. He sat up, rubbing his eyes, as the Bouncer came along.

"What! You back so soon?" he said.

"You said to come back in a year," the Bouncer replied, "and I would like a change from bouncing."

"He has been very good!" said the second magician. "He saved me when they were going to beat me."

"Oh well," said the first magician, "I suppose you can be a boy again, but you've got to walk from now on, not bounce."

He muttered his magic words backwards and there was the boy again, only his clothes were too small for him now because he was a year taller.

He thanked the magicians, and they went one way and he the other—all the way back home. His mother frowned at him when he came in.

"You're late!' she said. "Your dinner got cold and we had to give it to the cat."

"I've been bouncing round the world," said the boy. "It's made me pretty hungry."

"I'll make you a sandwich," she said. "But don't be so late again."

So that is the story of the boy who was turned into a Bouncer. He was always very careful when he walked about after that, in case he bounced on a magician.

Right~Hand Men

There was once a boy called Jack who was too small to go to school and too old to play with his baby sister. The trouble was that there were no other children for Jack to play with—not for miles—and he was often quite lonely. There was plenty to do on the farm where he lived, but the happiest part of doing things is sharing them with somebody else, and that is just what Jack missed most.

Sometimes he would go and talk with an old man who lived in a hut on a hill. Funnily enough the old man's name was Jack too, so there were a pair of them—Old Jack and Little Jack—talking together on the hillside. Old Jack told Little Jack stories of England where he had been born and of Australia and South America where he had lived for many years. This was often interesting and exciting, but it was only talking after all. You couldn't expect an Old Jack to go exploring the creek, or to go swinging out over the water on a creeper and falling in with a splash, or even to go climbing trees. He just sat and talked, screwing his eyes up at the sky, squinting at the clouds. Sometimes Little Jack felt Old Jack had forgotten all about him, and was just talking to the world.

One day Little Jack asked Old Jack a question.

"Did you have boys to play with when you were small, Jack?"

And then Old Jack turned his eyes away from the sky and looked at him thoughtfully.

"Why—yes! I had five!" he said at last.

"What were their names?" asked Little Jack curiously, because he liked to hear about other boys.

"They were the most curious set of boys I ever came across," said Old Jack, "and these were their names— Tommy Thumbkin, Billie Winkie, Long Duster, Jacky Molebar and Little Perky."

Little Jack's mouth and eyes grew as round as rabbit holes.

"What names!" he cried, and he said them over and over with Old Jack correcting him until he knew them by heart.

"They had lots of names," said Old Jack. "Other places call them by different ones, according to what place it is, but this is what we called them in Cheshire, where I was born."

"What were they like?" asked Little Jack. "How old were they?"

"As to age I couldn't rightly say," said Old Jack. "Though mostly they were my age and not a moment more or less—they were what you might call my right-hand men. Tommy Thumbkin—he was a short serious sort of boy, brave as a lion mind you, but a bit different from the others who were great ones for laughing. He used to whistle sweet as thrushes and blackbirds did Tommy, and wander off a bit on his own.

"Billie Winkie was a sailor boy with a tarry pigtail—for he wasn't a modern sort of sailor boy, but one of the old-fashioned sort that wore pigtails. He was strong and brown and had a funny rolling walk as if all the world was a ship deck. Long Duster—now he was a funny one—t-a-l-l," said Old Jack stretching the word out.

"T-a-l-l and gentle with long hair and a sad face. Even his laughing had something sad in it—mind you he wasn't sad company at all. He was great on the tree climbing because he had two great long arms on him. Jack Molebar—you'd have looked twice at him before you realized he was a boy because he was covered in black fur like a pussy-cat, only his face looking out, and a white tuft under his chin. Everything made him laugh—he was a really merry one.

"And as for Little Perky—he was a biscuit-coloured boy with foxy red hair, but the strangest things about him were his pricked-up ears, sharp like a smart little dog's always listening for the joke, and also his waving plumy tail."

"Tail!" said Little Jack. But Old Jack fell silent. "Gosh," said Little Jack, "I wish I'd known those boys."

"Well, so you do," Old Jack replied, "for they're

friends to every Jack that's born into this world with a thumb and four fingers. Look——" He took Little Jack's hand and said their names over slowly. "Tommy Thumbkin (that's your thumb), Billie Winkie (that's your first beckoning finger, you see). Long Duster (he's the longest finger you understand). Jacky Molebar (there's Jacky), and Little Perky (he's the smallest). Now when you see your right hand, for work or play you've got five fine friends to keep you company."

When Little Jack went off down the hill on the way home, he found he was not gone very far before someone put a furry paw into his hand and when he looked to the left—there was Jacky Molebar, and someone thumped him on the shoulder and there was Billie Winkie with sailor's earrings golden in his ears. Tall and slender and smiling shyly Long Duster looked down at him, and at his heels Little Perky laughed and danced and pulled funny foxy faces. And some distance away whistling shrill and sweet, Tommy Thumbkin nodded to him and waved a hand.

"You're real!" cried Little Jack. "You're not just pretending!"

"Oh, we're real all right," said Billie Winkie. "You just haven't been able to see us before because you didn't know we were here."

"But we were!" cried Jacky Molebar. "We were here all the time," and he laughed and turned head over heels so that dead leaves stuck to his black fur.

"You're covered in leafmould, mouldy old Jacky Molebar," screamed Little Perky, showing off, and he began a strange comical dance pulling such odd faces that they all laughed.

"We'll have lots of fun," murmured Tommy Thumbkin quietly. "The good times are coming."

19

But Long Duster looked at Little Jack and said, "I'm not surprised you didn't know whether we were real or not. I'm not quite sure myself."

"That's why he's so sad," Billie Winkie said, "but—why, I don't know anyone realler than we are—most people aren't half as real. And now for adventure."

What adventures they had that long golden summer. Little Jack didn't have time to stop and wonder whether or not his funny friends were real or just dreams. When they went exploring down the creek they found magical seas with islands in them. They were shipwrecked lots of times and once they were captured by pirates. Fortunately Tommy Thumbkin got free and helped them escape. They fought the pirates with swords, drove them off their ship onto an island and left them there. Billie Winkie sailed the pirate ship round all the islands and they found enough treasure and parrots and monkeys for them all to have some. They hunted lions in the jungle, fought great battles with blood-thirsty enemies, built castles as high as clouds, and rescued each other from all sorts of great dangers. Things were quite different for Little Jack when Tommy Thumbkin, Billie Winkie, Long Duster, Jacky Molebar and Little Perky went adventuring with him.

Then one day Jack's mother told him his cousin Alan was coming to stay. Jack told his five friends and they were all very excited though Long Duster seemed a little uncertain.

"There's those that don't like us," he said. "Suppose your cousin Alan is one of them."

"Of course he'll like us," squeaked Little Perky. "Aren't we the finest set of fellows we know? He'll love us."

When Alan came he turned out to be an ordinary boy, very friendly and pleased with the country, and slightly older than Jack. He was five years old and going to school. There was never a boy browner or sturdier than Alan. Somehow he was very real.

The strange thing was that he did not seem to see Jack's five funny friends or take any sort of notice of them at first. He listened to Jack talk about them and talk to them, with a puzzled face, sometimes a scornful face, as if he didn't understand all that was going on and did not like what he did understand. Then suddenly he said:

"I can see them now, those boys you're talking to Jack, those right-hand men." Jack saw Alan smile in a grown-up way as he said this, and he looked quickly at his right-hand men to see if they were at all worried by the smile. It struck him that they looked somehow dim and far away, almost as if their colours had been washed out. They smiled and nodded to him, but Long Duster's smile was very sad and for a moment Jack felt sad too. Then Alan said:

"Come on—let's play down in the creek," and off they all went, hunting a fierce rare animal with a horse's body and a lion's head and a snake's tail. They tracked it for miles—or so it seemed to Jack—and then came the catching of it. Alan wanted to gallop after it on horses and lassoo it, but Jacky Molebar wanted to dig a pit with nets of flax at the bottom and then chase the animal into the pit. Jack explained to Alan and then Alan said a funny thing.

"Yes, but we don't have to do what he says do we. He isn't real. He's just pretending isn't he?"

Jack stood still and behind him he felt the right-hand men waiting and listening and watching him hard. In front of him Alan watched and waited too, brown and real —really real.

"Isn't he?" Alan said again. "You know he's just make-up."

21

"Yes—I s'pose he is," Jack said slowly. "They're all just a game really."

He blinked his eyes and looked around. Where was furry Jacky Molebar now? Where were Tommy Thumbkin, Billie Winkie and foxy Little Perky? They were all gone. Only Long Duster lingered for a moment still smiling sadly at Jack.

"You see?" he said. "I thought we weren't real." And he waved his thin hand and went out like a candle. Jack stood staring after him.

"Come on!" Alan said impatiently. "I'll tell you

what, though! We'll leave them here to look after the camp and you and me'll ride after that animal and catch it by ourselves with our lassoos. Say those others sleep in and don't come with us."

"All right then," said Jack because there was nothing else to say, and off he went with Alan galloping after the strange animal.

Alan stayed all the Christmas holidays, and then in February Jack was five and went to school. So he wasn't ever lonely again, and didn't really have time to wonder what had become of his right-hand men until one Saturday, a long long time later, he told Old Jack all about it. Old Jack nodded slowly.

"Just the same with me," he grumbled. "They off and left me when I made other friends. That's the way with the right-hand men."

"Where have they gone?" asked Little Jack.

"Off to find some other Jack—a Jack-be-nimble or a Jack-o'dandy—it doesn't matter which——" said Old Jack "——but a lonely Jack somewhere's needing friends. They'll be climbing trees this minute or building forts in the bracken, or maybe digging for treasure. Who can say?"

And he screwed up his eyes at the blue sky, and waved his hand to the sun so that the long shadows of his five fingers danced over the bright grass.

23

The Road
to School

One day Teddy's mother had to go out for the morning and could not take Teddy. Because of this, it was specially arranged that Teddy could go to school with his brother Gerard—but just for the morning.

So this day in spring Teddy and Gerard went off to school together. It was just ordinary for Gerry, but for Teddy it was a new strange morning and he looked out at its pale blue and gold with interest and wonder. He wore neat clothes and had a playlunch of an apple, and even two sandwiches, because his mother did not know quite when she would be calling to collect him.

As she kissed them goodbye their mother looked into their eyes, and saw that Teddy's eyes were wide and brown and serious, but that Gerry's were excited like happy blue water, and secrets like mermaids were swimming in them.

"Funny Gerry!" she said, hugging him. "What are you thinking?"

Gerry just laughed and shook his head. But as they went out through the gate, beginning the mile walk to the school, Gerry said to Teddy: "Now you will meet my friends!"

"At school?" Teddy asked.

"No, on the way there," Gerry replied.

Well, it was spring, and the poplars were blushing green with it, and the hills were misty, soft and dreamy. Down where their own road crossed the main road, a

breeze sprang up as they went by, and twirled in the dust.
The dust rose until it was Teddy-high, in a little whirling,
furry grey cone, like a spinning top.

"Here's my first friend," said Gerry. Teddy peered at
the whirling dust, and just for a moment he saw a strange
face look out from it, then duck back again—a little grey
face with a slanting, sideways look, and he knew someone
was in there who did not want to be seen.

"Gerry," the dust said in a furry, furtive voice, "who
is that with you?"

"My brother Teddy," Gerry said proudly. "He's
going to school with me—but just for this morning."

"Ah, ah," said the far-away voice. "School is it?
That's the place for learning isn't it? That's where you
learn the words and the dance of them isn't it?"

"We have spelling and writing sentences," Gerry said
uncertainly.

"Well, a first day must be a special day," the dust

murmured on. "So I will give you a gift. It's not the bigness or the brightness of it you must go by, but the way it flowers when the right words are spoken." Then a thin arm, and a hand that was half a paw, and half a claw, snaked out, and dropped into Gerry's hand a small glass tube of sand. And then the wind died down, and the dust died down, and there was nothing at all.

"Who was that?" asked Teddy.

"I don't know his real name," Gerry replied, "but I call him the Little Grey Whirling Fellow, and he is made utterly all of dust."

So they went on their way.

Yes, it was spring, and the farmhouses had put on their dancing frocks of pink and white fruit blossom, and maybe, when the people were asleep, they danced up the valley and down the valley, all wild and glad with the spring.

"Here's another friend," Gerry said. Teddy peered up into a barberry tree and found that it wasn't a tree at all, but a man with his legs rooted into the ground, branching arms held high, green and growing, over his head. From his temples sprouted flowering barberry tree antlers. His face looked down brownly and secretly at Teddy.

"The Little Gerard!" he said. "And who is this?"

"Teddy, my brother," Gerry answered, "going to school with me, but just for the morning."

"I thought you were a tree," Teddy remarked.

"I don't know what I am," the tree-man said thoughtfully. "Once I was a man, but an old brown tattooed woman bewitched me to be rooted here like a tree. I make a good tree though, and I was a poor sort of man—cruel and mean, and unhappy of course. Yet, when I found myself here, bound and branching, everything came right for me.

26

I stretched my arms up to the sun, I pushed my roots deep into the warm, rich, brown earth, my misery flowed away and gladness came into me with the sunshine—and peace too."

"He *likes* being a tree," Gerry said in a pleased voice to Teddy.

"So it is your first day at school," the tree-man went on. "Today, once again, spring lifts my heart, and besides a first day should be a special day, so I shall give you a gift." With one twiggy, thorny hand he dropped a blue seed into Teddy's brown curled paw, and then he turned his face up to drink the sunlight.

"What is his name?" Teddy asked as they moved off down the road.

"I call him Just Barberry because that is the kind of tree he is," Gerry replied. The boys stopped where the road passed over a culvert, and a little muddy stream flowed out under their feet. They could see their reflections in the dark velvety water. Gerry whistled.

"I have another friend," he said.

Then almost frighteningly the smooth curtain of water tore apart, and a head covered in green, slimy waterweed, dripping wet and wild, came out. But Teddy saw at a glance that this time it was just an ordinary bog-woman such as you might find anywhere.

"Who's he?" she asked Gerry abruptly.

"He's Teddy, my brother, and he's going to school, just for this morning."

"Ah well," she muttered, nodding at Teddy, "you won't like it much, but I suppose you've got to go."

"Little Grey Whirling Fellow and Just Barberry said it was a special day and gave us presents," Teddy remarked cunningly.

"Them!" the bog-woman exclaimed, her nostrils curling with scorn. She pulled something shining out of her hair. "I'll give you a gift too, but just because you've got eyes the same colour as my boggy little stream here." Gerry scrambled down the bank. "What is it?" Teddy asked him when he got back on to the road.

"Just a bottle of water!" Gerry said. "Never mind! We'll wait and see, because you can't be at all sure of gifts, from such in-between people as they are."

And Gerry was right because—but the story is bolting away too fast. Gerry's school was a small one, and there was only one teacher. There were twenty-five children of all ages from five to seven and all kinds of sizes. While the teacher taught some of them the others worked away by themselves. But you couldn't help overhearing what was going on sometimes, and Gerry (and Teddy beside him) heard the teacher telling the older children about Africa.

"It has great deserts too," the teacher was saying, "especially in the north."

At that very moment there came a pop and a tinkle of glass. The tube of sand Little Grey Whirling Fellow had given them burst, and the sand ran out. But so much sand! It flowed everywhere pushing away the walls of the schoolhouse. Then the chimney turned into a date palm, and there they were—a school of children and their teacher all on their own in the desert.

"This is most gratifying!" the teacher said, in delight. "We shall all be able to profit by this."

Then from behind a date palm came an Arab in flowing robes and he led twenty-six camels, one as white as a moonbeam. The Arab bowed to the teacher. "Ah! Excellent!" the teacher cried. "And I shall have that white one!" he added.

Ah—the desert—the silent rosy morning, and the camels padding across rippled sand—the fantastic domed cities, jewelled and forbidden—the sandstorms—the cold clear nights—none of them would ever forget these things. How long were they there? Who can say! They seemed to ride for days and days. But then, suddenly came cries and the shooting of guns. Wild Arabs were upon them, riding horses as black as thunder, as red as fire. "Quick, children, into that pyramid!" the teacher shouted. So they rode their camels into a nearby pyramid . . . and lo and behold, the camels became their desks, and the pyramid was the schoolroom.

"Well, that was very educational," declared the teacher, shaking the sand out of his trouser turnups. "But I see it is only 10 a.m., so I will take Group Three for spelling."

29

The surprises weren't over yet, for the first word he asked them to spell was "Jungle". Then the blue seed heard and popped open—out came the creepers and trees, with great glossy green leaves—out came butterflies with painted, glowing wings—out came flowers as big as cupped hands, all crimson, and golden and dripping with honey. The school sprouted and grew upward, and there they were . . . twenty-five children and a teacher in the jungle.

"This is very fortunate," the teacher observed. "Children, the jungle is all around us. Notice please that it is spelt JUNGLE. Now we shall see what we can learn.".

They seemed to be there many hot burning days and dark, warm nights. They saw humming birds and monkeys, wild spotted leopards and herds of elephants with pale moony tusks. And at last they came to a city made entirely of ivory, so magical and strange they scarcely dared to tread its lost streets or look in its empty windows. But as they stood, half bewitched, a hundred tigers with orange-and-black striped coats, and eyes like chinky emeralds, sprang after them.

"Quick, children, in here!" the teacher called, pushing them into a black doorway, and nobly being the last man in. But twink! It was their schoolroom and only 11 a.m.

"Life is full of surprises," the teacher remarked, mopping his brow, "but few are as pleasant as that one. Still, we must press on. Group One, I will now hear your reading. Gerard, will you begin?" Gerard began to read.

"The new word for today is Water," the teacher said, but as he spoke the lid of Gerard's desk flew open, the cork burst out of the bog-woman's bottle, and the water leaped up like a fountain. Indeed, less a fountain than a wave—it swept down on them, and then suddenly was sea-green. There they were . . . twenty-five children and a teacher deep under the sea, with fish like birds and butterflies around and above them, and seaweed spreading its lacy shawls before them.

"The new word, I repeat, is 'Water'," the teacher said firmly. "It is all around us at this moment."

A mermaid came by leading a school of merry dolphins. The teacher and the children each chose a dolphin to ride, and set out to make the sea their own.

There was a wonderful adventure in a world of silence and salt. They saw whole drowned kingdoms, sunken from the land, castles and kings and the shells of ships held in the scaly embrace of the sea serpents. And just as they dared to approach the loveliest ship of all, a golden galleon blooming with the strange flowers of the sea, a treasure of jewels spilling from her broken side onto the blue sand, they were horrified to see a hundred sharks, snaky-green and white, charging on them.

"Quick, children, into the ship!" the teacher called, and they swam over the side and onto the deck, down her companionway—and back into the schoolroom again . . . and it was only twelve o'clock.

"A most instructive morning," the teacher said wearily, "but very tiring." And when he went home for lunch, his wife was amazed to see him sandy from the desert, sunburned from the jungle, and salty from the sea.

"How did you like school?" Teddy's mother asked him later.

"Well, it was all right. . . ." Teddy said. "It was very special really!"

"It isn't always like that," Gerry said quickly.

"It's the road to school that's best," Teddy went on, yawning. "Because it's ours. The desert, and the jungle, and the sea aren't ours, but Little Grey Whirling Fellow, Just Barberry and the bog-woman . . . they're ours, aren't they, Gerry?"

The Thief and the Magic

There was once a grubby little hut in a wood, and here lived a thief with his mother who had once been a thief too. However, she got stiffness in the joints and creaked so much that it woke up everyone in the houses she was stealing from. Because of this she went into retirement, but she missed the old days. She used to grumble at her son.

"When I was young thieves were *thieves*—real craftsmen. We worked day and night at our stealing. But nowadays young thieves only think of the money. We were above that. We'd steal *anything*, just for the love of it."

"Yes, Ma," her young thief would say with a yawn. But mind you, this thief was very lazy, and when his mother told him to go out and steal, he'd always make some excuse and stay home in bed.

One day the thief's mother came into the room and said, "We've run out of butter and cheese and money. Hadn't you better do some stealing?"

"Can't we eat turnips instead?" the thief asked, but his mother was determined. The thief knew he'd have to get up and steal something. Also, he was quite a kind-hearted thief and hated to disappoint his old creaking mother.

"I won't have to go far," he said. "There's that cabin over the hill. Someone's living there now, and no doubt they will have some cheese and butter and money."

The path over the hill was shining and the hill itself was all golden green in the early summer sun. If the thief had been a poet he could have written a poem, but as it was, his head was full of plans for stealing. He hid behind a tree and watched the cabin. The someone who lived there was a raggedy little man. The thief saw him brush his teeth, then clean his boots, and then the raggedy man went out, walking like a shadow right past the tree where the thief was hiding. Then the thief came out and went down to the cottage. The door was not locked—actually it was wide open. Either the little ragged man was too poor to be scared of robbers, or he had a trusting nature. The thief, stealing-bag in hand, looked around the cabin. It was very bare. There were a mop and a broom and a pair of gum-boots behind the door and, hanging from nails in the wall, two long scarves—two *very* long scarves, in fact—one blue and one red. There were two boxes and a suitcase. This was all the furniture in the room. The thief opened his stealing-bag, and began stealing. He stole a nutmeg grater and a fish slice. He stole bread and cheese and jam too. He stole a calendar because he liked the picture on it.

Then he got a surprise. Something moved in the corner of the room—sat up and scratched itself. The thief had thought it was a sack, old and unravelling, but it was a dog. It looked more like a tattered sack than a dog, however, so it wasn't the thief's fault he had not realized. The dog finished scratching and lay down again, watching the thief with sharp black eyes.

"Good dog," said the thief, but it took all the fun out of his stealing to know someone was watching him. He took a candle in a half-hearted way, put it in his bag, and made for the door.

Then something strange happened. Music began to come into the air—twangling, out-of-tune-sounding music. It rose and fell, chased itself, lost its place and went wandering. Out from behind the door came the mop and the broom dancing a solemn and stiff little dance, bowing and shaking their hair. "*Ting-tang-tong*" went the twangling music and the mop and broom began to dance in a circle round the thief. The gumboots began to shuffle and then to stamp and then to do a kicking Russian dance in the corner. The thief watched the boots uneasily for a moment. Then he looked back to the mop and the broom. Somehow they had unhooked the two scarves and were doing a scarf dance, swaying and twisting, winding in and out of their own scarves and out of each other too. The scarves made red-and-blue loops and waves and coils in the shadows of the little hut.

"Ahem," said the thief, clutching his stealing-bag to his chest. "Thank you I'm sure." He wanted to please the mop and broom but he couldn't clap then because his

hands were full of stealing-bag. He bowed instead, as they
pirouetted on their single legs, and then he made for the
open door. Then the dog sat up. All at once the mop and
broom made a little rush at him. They looped the scarves
round and round him until he was more like a blue-and-
red cocoon than a man. When he was bound hand and foot
and could move no more, they bowed back to him and went
to their places behind the door, where they leaned themselves against the door, stiff and still. From its corner the
dog watched him keenly.

The thief lay and blinked. There was nothing he could

do about anything. At least, since the scarves were made of wool, he was very warm, but he could not escape.

After a while there was the sound of rustling feet and the raggedy little man came in at the door. The dog got up and went to meet him, wagging its tail.

"Oh," said the little ragged man in surprise. "A thief." He went down on his knees and began to unknot and unwind the scarves.

"Yes, sir!" said the thief sharply, as soon as he could. "I am a respectable thief, and let me tell you, this is not what I am used to!"

"I'm very sorry," said the raggedy man humbly.

"If I had known you were a magician," the thief went on, "I wouldn't have come here."

"But I'm not a magician," said the raggedy man. "I'm just a tramp called Jumping Bean. It's my dog who is a magician." The dog smiled at the thief and wagged its tail as if it was a wand. "Is this yours?" Jumping Bean asked, picking up the stealing-bag.

"Yes," said the thief. He added sulkily, "I suppose you'll want your things back again."

Jumping Bean peered into the bag. "Only the fish slice," he said. "Not the other things, and we don't use the nutmeg grater. We don't like nutmeg."

The thief was now free.

"Well," he said, "I must say, magician or not, I'd never wish to steal from the house of a finer fellow than yourself. You've been fair—very fair, and I don't mind giving you back your fish slice."

"Ah well," said Jumping Bean, "I like to help a fellow creature on his way."

So with these words of mutual esteem the thief and the tramp parted. The thief went home to his creaking mother to boast of his stealing. But Jumping Bean and his dog sat down to eat a fine roast duck with orange sauce which the dog magicked up, because, let me tell you, that dog was a *real* magician!

The Merry~Go~Round

There was once a fair travelling from town to town. Such a gay fair, with balloons and fortune-tellers, and candy floss and peanuts: with monkeys, performing dogs, a fat lady and a mermaid. You have probably seen lots of fairs like it.

But the prettiest thing of all in the fair was a merry-go-round with ten prancing horses. Each horse had a flowing mane and tail of real horsehair, a fine arching neck and swift galloping hoofs. They went round and round under a roof painted with new moons, with comets, and with silver far-away stars, so that the children who rode on them could look up and imagine they were frisking at night into a dark blue and silver sky.

The two men who owned the merry-go-round were called Todd and Barney. It was Todd who had carved the horses and made their proud, red leather saddles, but it was Barney who started the motor and who oiled it and greased it and kept it purring softly. It needed to be very soft because, once the motor was going steadily, Barney would pick up his brown violin, and play the merriest dancing music you ever heard, while Todd kept time with him hitting little strips of metal with a special tiny hammer. It sounded like fairy music—a fiddle and

gentle chiming bells, heard on a summer day. And all the time the engine went CHUG, chug, chug, CHUG, chug, chug in the background, and the horses went round and round bowing and rocking in a stately dance.

The trouble was that Barney and Todd were not good business men. When they saw that the children were enjoying their ride, Barney would wink and Todd would nod, and off the children would go for another three minutes without paying any extra. Then when the master of the fair came round at the end of the day and Barney and Todd had to give him half the money they had earned—why, the master would pull a very long face and say:

"Is that all?"

"That's all," Todd would say, looking uncomfortable.

"Have you been giving free rides again?" the master would ask.

"Just a few!" Barney would mutter. "But the children loved it."

Then the master would say, "When will you learn that business is business? Free rides don't earn you your living." And he would stump off.

One day they came to quite a new town by a dark wood, and there the fair set itself up—peanuts, monkeys, mermaid and all. Barney and Todd were there too. Off went the horses, off went Barney on the violin and off went Todd on the bells. As they played Todd saw a little boy walk out of the wood and stand there, watching them. His eyes were like deep brown pools in a bush creek.

When the music and the horse's dance were ended Todd said, "Would you like a ride, son?"

42

"I haven't any money!" said the boy in a small thin voice. Todd winked at Barney, and Barney nodded to Todd.

"Hop on, son," said Todd, "and we'll give you a spin for nix." Which meant a free ride for the brown-eyed boy. Round and round he went, and his eyes glowed, and the brown horse he rode went in sweeping free bounds as if at any moment it might break free, and fly over the wood on its own. After the ride the boy thanked them and Todd saw him run back into the wood.

"That's a funny thing," he said to Barney. "He must live there."

"There's no law against that, is there?" asked Barney.

"No, but I wonder what it would be like to live in a wood?" Todd said. "It might be a happy place to live."

"Or it might be wet!" said Barney, starting the engine up again.

The day went by just as you might expect for a merry-go-round at a fair, but that evening, just as Barney and Todd had finished packing their merry-go-round onto the back of their little green van, they heard a great noise and a roaring of wheels, and in to the fair came a big truck, and on the side of the truck was painted "Mercury Merry-Go-Rounds Ltd".

"Mercury Merry-Go-Round?" cried Barney. "What does this mean? Don't they know that this fair has a merry-go-round already?"

"I'll tell you what it means!" cried the fair master, suddenly popping up beside them. "It means the end of free rides, the end of violins and bells, the end of Barney and Todd and their ten prancing horses. You aren't earning enough money, so I have sent for a new merry-go-round. Its horses swing out fierce and far, and it has fine, loud music on a gramophone and loud-speakers. And its owner will never allow any free rides. He is a business man. As for you, I don't want to see you or hear your miserable CHUG, chug, chug machine again. My word, you should hear how the engine of my new merry-go-round roars.

44

And, roaring with noisy laughter, the fair master stumped away.

That evening, when the fair left town, it left behind it Barney and Todd, sadly sitting on the running board of their van.

Over the hill the moon rose round and bright, but Barney and Todd still sat there. They had nowhere to go. Then beside them a shadow stirred. They turned round, and there was the boy from the wood. He was quite bare, except for a kilt of green, and a garland of starry white flowers in his hair.

"Here, you should be in bed!" said Barney, startled. "What's your mother thinking of, letting you out this time of night?"

The boy fixed his bright eyes on them.

"Barney and Todd," he said, "there's more kinds of business in the world than making money. So take me into your van with you, and drive where I tell you and you won't lose by it."

"Here, there's something funny about this . . ." began Barney.

But Todd said, "Go on, Barney, be a sport. Maybe the kid's got a party on somewhere and we can liven it up a bit for him." So the three of them got into the van, and the boy directed them into the wood. It was not easy to drive there at night, yet Barney seemed to find it no trouble at all.

"It seems as if the trees are making way for me," he said.

"When you have one of the wood people with you," the boy replied, "all ways are open to you."

Then Barney and Todd looked at the boy, and saw

that he was indeed one of the wood people—people who live with the trees and moss and fern, and hide from the eyes of the world.

"See what you've let us in for now," groaned Barney.

But Todd said, "Go on with you, maybe our luck's on the turn."

At last they arrived in a clear moonlit place surrounded by trees.

"Put up your merry-go-round here," the boy told them, "and we'll see what we shall see."

So there in the moonlight a strange scene took place. Barney and Todd set up their merry-go-round. Todd talked to the horses as he polished their saddles and combed their manes. Then Barney pulled the starter rope and off went the engine—CHUG, chug, chug, off went the horses, off went Barney on the violin, off went Todd on the bells. The black and silver glade was filled with the beat and melody of Barney and Todd's merry-go-round. As they played both Barney and Todd first felt the gaze of many eyes upon them, and then saw a shadowy line forming as the wood people came out to watch and wonder. When Barney stopped the engine, and the horses slowed down, these strange people, these midnight people, came forward and climbed silently onto the horses' backs. They didn't shout and laugh like the children, and Barney and Todd found it hard to see them. They caught the gleam of eyes, and heard a sound like the wind in leaves, but nobody said anything to them, nobody questioned them.

All night Barney and Todd worked their merry-go-round in the moonlit glade until they fell asleep in the early morning. When they woke up the boy was standing there with a bowl of milk and a bowl of fruit.

"Stay and play for the wood people tonight," he said, "and you will go neither hungry nor thirsty."

Barney and Todd stayed in the wood for some time, sleeping during the day, and working their merry-go-round at night to the shadowy wood people who came and went, saying not a please or a thank you.

"They're not what you'd call cheerful," grumbled Barney, "not a laugh or a smile in the whole lot of them."

"I miss the kids and the fun of the fair," agreed Todd, "but there you are—it's a living, isn't it?"

Then one day their friend the boy came to them bringing a big poster. "This was stuck on a telegraph pole just out of town," he said. "I thought you'd like to see it."

Barney and Todd stared at it. It read:

GREAT MERRY-GO-ROUND
COMPETITION
A merry-go-round competition will be held on the fair-ground. The winner will be given a thousand pounds and the title of "The world's most wonderful merry-go-round". All merry-go-rounds may enter. Everybody come!

"It's today!" cried Todd. "Let's hurry, Barney. Boy, thank you for showing us this. We will come back and play for you tonight, but we would like to enter this grand merry-go-round contest."

47

"And so you shall," the boy said. "Look at your merry-go-round! While you slept the wood people have painted it for you again, and combed the manes and tails of your horses. Now we are going to teach you a tune to play. It will bring you good luck."

And the boy hummed a strange little song. Barney soon learned to play it on his violin, and Todd beat it out on the bells. All around they felt as if the people of the wood were listening and watching and wishing them luck.

"Do you know it now?" asked the boy. "Don't forget it, and off you go, and we wood people hope you will do well."

As they left the glade in their green van Barney and Todd saw the air shine and sparkle as if it was full of fire-flies. They heard a misty sound like the echo of pipes and bells. It was the first sound they had heard from the shadowy wood people. It was the wood people laughing. Barney and Todd looked out into the shine and the shadow and laughed too. Their laughing made its own sparkle in the soft dark under the trees. Probably no one else in the world had laughed and sparkled with the people of the wood.

Well, the fair-ground was crowded with merry-go-rounds of all sizes. But they were all bigger and gaudier and louder than the little merry-go-round of Barney and Todd. Ten children were chosen to judge the merry-go-rounds, and all day they went round and round and round, sometimes higher, sometimes faster, sometimes noisier, with rests in between because they were so giddy. At last, in the evening, they came to the little merry-go-round of Barney and Todd.

"Ha, ha, ha!" roared the other merry-go-round owners. "What a sight! They won't get much fun out of that one."

"Ho, ho, ho!" sniggered the fair owners. "I wouldn't have them on *my* fair-grounds."

But the children noticed the beautiful prancing horses and the wonderful colours that seemed to glow and shine. They climbed into the comfortable, polished, red leather saddles. In the late afternoon light the eyes of the horses looked alive.

49

Then Barney pulled the starting rope. CHUG, chug, chug—off went the engine, off went the horses, off went Barney on the violin and off went Todd on the bells. They played the tune of the wood people.

Then out from the ears of the horses came blue and white butterflies in clouds, out from under the bow of Barney's violin came flocks of blue birds and dragonflies. Up round the centre of the merry-go-round grew leaves and grapes and white flowers, so that the children could reach out and pick them as they went past. The blue starry roof went up and up and spread all over the sky and the new moon, comets and stars frolicked together. And, last of all, the ten horses grew rainbow-coloured wings and flew up and up, to dance among the stars. When at last the tune came to an end, and the horses came back to earth and the butterflies, birds, grapes and flowers vanished, the children got off and shouted that Barney and Todd had won first prize.

Now Barney and Todd were rich and famous, and all the fair-owners wanted their merry-go-round to work for them. But:

"No!" said Barney.

"No!" said Todd.

They set off on their travels again with their thousand pounds. For half the year they go from town to town giving children free rides on their ten prancing horses, and for half the year they work at night in the woods of the world, playing to the wood people who come silently out of the shadows to listen and to ride.

And sometimes, when the day is summery and blue, or the wind is in the north, or for no reason at all except that they feel like it, they play the tune of the wood people and those are the most wonderful merry-go-round rides in the world. If you are lucky you might have such a ride when Barney and Todd come to your town, and you need not pay anything except a smile, or a thank you, or a laugh or a kiss.

Kite Saturday

Today was Kite Saturday. Today was the day when the children took their kites up into the hills and set them flying—strange, bright birds in a pale sky. John ran and Dick ran, Sally, Lilly and Marigold ran. From under their arms streamed raggle-taggle kite tails bowing and dancing to a secret music. Every child had a kite and every kite had a child. Together they bobbed and ran to the hills, which were free and windy and wide enough to hold them all.

Behind all the other children ran Joan. Her fingers were too clumsy to make a kite, to cut and glue the paper and stretch the string. She did not have a father or brother to do this for her. However, hard and round in the palm of her hand she had a fivepenny piece which her mother had given her.

"Get yourself a little treat," she said, for she knew Joan was disappointed at having no kite to fly. For five pence Joan could buy an ice-cream cone or a glass of orange juice. For five pence she could buy a pink sugar mouse, with a tail of green angelica. A silver piece has its own silver magic. Still, on Kite Saturday a kite is the most magical thing of all.

On the last corner in town an old woman sat beside

a straw basket, watching the children stream past to the hills. No child but Joan saw her because the autumn wind ran in front of them wearing a pied cloak made of red and yellow leaves, and they were following the wind. No child but Joan read the notice on her straw basket—"Lucky-Dip. Wishes and Dreams".

Joan stopped. "Is it *really* wishes and dreams?" she asked the old woman.

"You have to pay a silver piece to find out, you see," the old woman said. She smoked a pipe, this old woman —and her eyes were as still and grey as stones. She puffed out blue smoke, and watched Joan through it.

"*Everyone* would want to dip," said Joan.

"Ah, yes, but I go only to the lonely places," said the old woman, "or places where people are hurrying past me."

"You can't get many silver pieces that way," said Joan.

"No, but the ones I do get are special ones," the old woman told her.

Joan held out her silver piece and the old woman took it. She looked at it, bit it and smiled a little.

"You may have a dip!" she said.

The lucky-dip smelled of hay and sawdust. Joan wriggled her fingers down into it, feeling for a parcel. She felt first one and then another. She was just going to take the second one, when a third parcel pushed its way into her hand. It was as if that parcel was telling her "Take *me*! I'm the *special* one." So Joan took it. It was quite small and wrapped in silver paper.

"Don't open it until you get to the hills," the old woman said. "That's a parcel that needs space."

"It's only a little one," Joan remarked.

"It still needs space," the old woman replied sternly. "A certain herd of elephants might live contentedly in a walnut shell, while a particular mouse might need all the space between the stars."

Joan did not understand what the old woman was saying.

"I'm going to watch the kites fly," she said. "I'll open it in the hills."

But the old woman merely put her pipe back in her mouth and rested her elbows on her knees and her chin in her hands. Her eyes stared out of her brown face much like stones that are half buried in the earth stare always up to the stars.

Up in the hills the children were getting ready to fly their kites. The wind came down the slopes to meet them, head over heels, tumbling like an acrobat and laughing like a clown. It lifted the first kites high into the air and higher still. All the time it piped among the rocks, full of conceit at its own cleverness.

Sitting on a smooth stone, warm in the sun, Joan opened her silver parcel. As she turned back the last folds, something struggled and moved, something opened up under her hands.

It was a kite Joan was holding! A kite which had unfolded from her lucky-dip parcel. It was taller than Joan herself, and had for a tail a chain of leaves and berries and flowers. Painted on its green silk was a wild laughing face, such as the wind itself might wear.

The other children were flying their kites now. Their

lines stretched through the air like the strings of a great fiddle—one only the wind could play. The wind was delighted to see Joan's big kite and came eagerly to meet her.

"Look at Joan's kite!" a child called. "It's the biggest of all."

"Look at Joan's kite!" the other children shouted. "It's going higher and higher."

The wind lifted the kite.

It lifted Joan too.

Joan was not afraid. She felt quite safe. The smell of autumn, of falling leaves and sun-warmed grass, rose around her as she soared up the clear hill of the air, dangling on the silver string of her kite. Then the wind brought her, like a little extra present, the sharp salt smell of the sea.

The hill opened up beneath her like green flowers, and suddenly she could see over them. She could see to the very edge of the world. Between Joan and the hills and the edge of the world was a blue field where lines of white unicorns charged and danced. No—it wasn't a blue field . . . it was the sea, and the white unicorns were tossing waves.

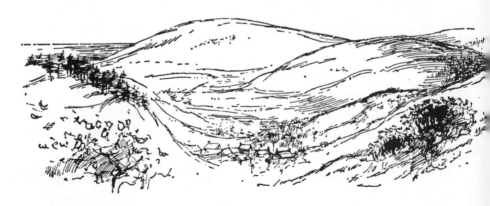

"Wishes and dreams!" said the wind. "Wishes and dreams."

It was Kite Saturday and a beautiful day.

But even Kite Saturday must end. Even the wind gets tired. Falling with the autumn leaves, down came the kites out of the sky. Down came Joan on the end of her silvery string. She felt the grass under her feet. Fluttering and bowing her kite slid down behind her, dancing while it could, watching her with eyes as golden as an owl's.

The other children crowded round her.

"What did it feel like, flying?" they asked her, but Joan could not exactly tell them.

"A bit like floating—a bit like swinging, just before you swing down again. From up in the air the hills were like green flowers, and over the hills I could see the sea."

Suddenly the wind leaped up and away from them, shouting and clapping its hands and turning cartwheels from one hill top to another. He had forgotten the children and their kites. He was playing his own secret games again. Tired and happy, the children sighed and smiled and turned home, with the kite tails hanging quietly over their arms.

Kite Saturday was over.

The Witch Doctor

There was once a young man called Tom whose father was a doctor and he wanted Tom to be a doctor too.

Tom did not want to be a doctor. He wanted to write poetry.

All day, all night, words sang in his thoughts like birds in a forest. When the wind blew Tom heard a giant shouting enchanted words of power. When the sun shone Tom tried to shine too, speaking out strong golden words.

Tom should have been a poet BUT "You must be a doctor too," said his father. "Those are my orders." Tom had to turn round and study to be a medical man. Poor Tom!

"What is this?" said the professor who was teaching the young men to be doctors. "Someone has written me a poem. I wanted a list of different sorts of bones."

"Well," said Tom, "I could not remember the names of the bones."

"If someone came to you with a broken leg, would you read him a poem?" said the professor with great and dreadful scorn.

"Well, it might be better than nothing," said Tom. "And people have dreams as well as bones."

"Young man," said the professor, "you will never make a doctor. It is people's bones you should think of, not their dreams."

But Tom worked hard.

He learned all the bones.

He learned all the muscles.

He made songs of them and sang them to himself until he knew them by heart.

After several goes he passed the exam.

At last, Tom became a doctor.

The trouble was, Tom was not a very good doctor.

Nothing he did turned out well.

He got his medicines mixed up. He got spots and swellings mixed up too. He gave chicken-pox people measles medicine. He gave mumps people lumps medicine.

When he should have been reading books about stomach-aches Tom was writing poetry.

After a while no one came to him unless they wanted him to write a poem for the birthday of some rich aunt.

Tom did not charge for a poem. He thought poetry should be free.

One night he sat at home just starving and writing poetry. It was a cold night, and there were cracks in the walls of his old house. He had many of the cracks covered by poems pasted on the wall and the poems helped to keep him warm. Tom wrote busily.

"Up in a meadow close to the sea
  Girls in bright dresses came dancing with me."

He pulled his coat round him and imagined the

meadow by the sea, the hot, hot sunshine, the tall blue flowers and the girls in their swirling skirts, like summer butterflies. The meadow seemed more real than the cold room with poems pasted all over the walls.

Tom smiled. Just as he smiled there was a loud ring at his doctor's bell on the front door.

Tom opened the door. There stood an old woman as sharp as a thorn. She wore a pointed hat and a black cloak. She carried an enormous besom broom. Even in the light of his candle Tom could see that she was very plain and spattered with spots.

"Are you the doctor?" she asked.

"Yes," said Tom, "I am a doctor, but I must warn you that I'm not a very good one."

The old woman peered at him.

"You don't look very good," she agreed. "How are you with spots? I want you to cure mine."

"What's wrong with them?" asked Tom cautiously.

"Can't you see!" snapped the old woman. "They ruin my beauty."

"Oh no!" said Tom politely. "True beauty always shines through any number of spots."

The old woman simpered. "Oh well, no doubt you're right," she said, "but I demand to be cured of them all the same. No girl likes to share her face with a lot of spots."

"I can't promise anything," Tom stammered, thinking sadly of his sunny dream, the bright girls and the leaping sea. "I've never been very successful with spots."

The old woman bounced in Tom's door like a wicked black frog.

"You'd better be successful with mine," she said, "or I'll want to know the reason why."

She spoke in a very ominous voice, a crackling, spitting voice, as if she was frying her words in very hot fat.

Tom jumped back as if he had been stung.

He started mixing up some medicine. "Now was

it that pink powder that was so good for spots, or was it that blue fizzy stuff," he muttered. He mixed away with shaking hands.

He mixed a tall purple medicine for the spotty old woman. It smelled terrible.

"I wish I felt sure it would work," Tom muttered.

But the old lady snatched it from him and swigged it down with a flick and a swish. It sounded like bath water gurgling down a plughole.

"Very tasty!" she said at last, smacking her lips.

It was at this very moment Tom remembered something. Horrible horrors! That blue fizzy stuff was meant for sprained ankles—not spots.

Tom turned cold all over. He wondered how he could explain this mistake, though it was a mistake any doctor who happened also to be a poet could make. He cleared his throat.

"Have you ever had a sprained ankle?" he asked.

But as he spoke he noticed a remarkable thing. The spots were fading.

They got smaller and smaller.

They vanished entirely.

Tom was astonished. It was the first time he had cured anybody of anything.

The old woman saw her reflection in the side of Tom's own whistling kettle. She leaped up with a joyous cry.

"Gone!" she exclaimed. "My radiant beauty has come back better than before."

She was highly delighted. She gave Tom a small bag of gold, and went off chuckling and telling Tom she would recommend him to her friends. Dr Tom was

left on his own. He looked hard at the bottle of blue
fizzy stuff. He looked hard at the bag of gold. Then he
shrugged his shoulders and went back to his poem. He
let sunshine creep around him once more, and in his
mind he danced with silken summer girls to the hush
and sigh of the sea.

It wasn't long before there came another ring on
his doctor's bell and another sharp old woman stood
there in a sharp hat and sharp shoes, with sharp eyes
peering back at him. She had a swollen face.

Tom cured her (with a lotion in which he mixed
gunpowder by mistake).

"Very good! Very good!" she said. "I haven't
known such medical success before. We witches find it
hard to get a doctor."

"Witches!" cried Tom amazed.

"Why yes—you're a natural-born witch doctor,
didn't you know? Medicine works backwards with

witches so a usual doctor isn't much good to us," said the witch.

She gave Tom a bag of gold and went out still patting her face.

"My radiant beauty has come back at last," Tom heard her saying as she went out.

Tom stood there uneasily. "I haven't heard the last of this," he thought.

Somehow he knew it was no use sitting down to write more poetry. His poetry was quite gone. He went to bed instead.

In the morning when Tom woke up he knew straight away that he was worried. It took him a moment to remember what he was worried about.

Witches! He had been curing witches.

He lay in bed and worried for five exact minutes. Then he thought, "Even a man who has been curing witches has to have breakfast."

He got up and set his breakfast table. Then he went to see what he had in his cupboard.

Well! Three lemons and a tin of sardines!

Not much for a man who has worn himself out the night before writing poetry and curing witches of spots.

Tom was considering, when a ring sounded on the doctor's bell. Tom frowned. Could it be another witch? Could it be the police? Did you get a chance to write poetry if you were put in prison for witch curing?

He went to the door and opened it boldly. There stood the beautiful Sabina.

"Sardines for breakfast?" she asked him, smiling.

"And for lunch," Tom answered, "and for dinner too."

Tom looked at her.

She had golden hair, but so pale a gold it was almost silver. She had blue eyes, but so dark a blue they were almost purple. She had a pink and white skin, and in the middle of her face a very red nose.

As Tom looked at her she sneezed twenty-seven times.

"I know you are good with spots and swellings," she said. "What are you like with sneezes?"

She was just so beautiful, in spite of her red nose, that Tom tried hard to think how to mix sneeze medicine. Meanwhile Sabina began to read all the poems pasted over the cracks in the walls. Her sneezing made quite a breeze and some poems blew off the walls. Soon the air was filled with whirling poetry.

Tom frowned and drummed his fingers. What was good for sneezes?

The beautiful Sabina blinked her purple eyes.

"You need a good housekeeper," she said. "I think I will come and housekeep for you."

"Then I must cure you," Tom replied, grinning a little bit. "I know," he said. "I'll make you a lemon drink with my three lemons. My medicine works only with the wrong people. A lemon drink will be as good as anything for you."

"You write interesting poetry," said the beautiful Sabina. "I like this one,

"Up in a—*Achoo!*—close to the sea
   Girls in bright—*achoos!*—come dancing with me."

"That isn't quite how I meant it to sound," said Tom.

He must have had a good way of squeezing lemons. He made a splendid three-lemon lemon drink which cured the sneezes straight away. Then the beautiful Sabina began tidying the house and Tom sat down and began writing poetry.

"Where did you get that broom?" Tom asked, looking up for a moment.

"Oh, I always bring my own with me," the beautiful Sabina answered.

A moment later when Tom was working out a very tricky rhyme for "hyena" there came a loud knocking at his door.

"Come out! Come out!" voices shouted. "We know what you've been up to. You've been curing witches!"

Tom sighed. "Real trouble this time," he said mournfully. Then he opened his door.

There stood the mayor, the councillors, the policeman and a crowd of people.

"*There* you are! *There* you are!" they shouted.

"You have been curing witches," said the mayor. "It is useless to deny it."

"Well, perhaps I have cured one or two," Tom admitted, "but I did not know they were witches."

"The witches round here," said the mayor, "are a very spiteful lot. And that is when they are merely poorly. Now they are well they will be a hundred times worse. There's no room in this town for a doctor who goes around curing witches. You will have to leave and we are here to make you go."

"But I can't leave this house," cried Tom. "All my poetry is pasted over the holes and cracks in the walls. I can't leave my collected writings behind."

An angry, ominous murmur rose from the people before him. "Get rid of him! Get rid of him!" they shouted. "Get that witch doctor out of town."

The policeman sprang up the steps and seized Tom by his shirt. Tom struggled but he had had no breakfast—not even sardines. The policeman had had eggs and bacon and a sausage, followed by toast and milky coffee and a kiss from his wife. He was feeling tremendously strong. There is no doubt he would have overwhelmed Tom and carried him off to jail, but something unexpected happened.

The beautiful Sabina came out of the door behind him. She was so beautiful that all that angry crowd grew quiet. The policeman stayed holding Tom up in the air.

"Good morning," said the beautiful Sabina. She smiled at them with her pink lips and her purple eyes. "What are you doing with Dr Tom?"

"We're chasing him out of town," said the mayor after a moment. "He's been curing witches."

"But that's wonderful!" said the beautiful Sabina. "You won't have any more trouble from witches now. Witches are quite amiable when they are feeling well."

Everyone stared at her.

The mayor shuffled his feet nervously. "Do you know that for a fact?" he asked. "I thought their wickedness would get worse."

"Oh no!" Sabina replied in a surprised voice. "When they are well, witches concentrate on cackling, dancing and having gay witch parties. Wickedness in witches often comes from spots or indigestion. Besides, now you have a witch doctor in town, witches will come from far and wide bringing trade with them. They will spend money in the shops, buying gay scarves, beads and other pretty trinkets."

The mayor looked thoughtful. He himself, when he was not being mayor, had a fancy-goods shop full of scarves, beads and trinkets.

"Perhaps we are being hasty," he said. "This wants looking into."

"We don't want to do anything rash," said a councillor.

"No," said the beautiful Sabina, "because if I was a witch—*if* I was a witch—I would be very angry to find a mayor and town council had chased a perfectly good witch doctor out of town."

The beautiful Sabina's voice sounded quite ominous, in a beautiful way, almost as if she just might really have been a witch herself.

"We'll have to have a meeting about this," said the mayor. "Constable, put that witch doctor down."

They marched off, leaving Tom and the beautiful Sabina staring after them.

The beautiful Sabina beckoned Tom into the kitchen. There, in the middle of the table, was a big three-tier-top cake wonderfully iced and decorated with lilies and roses made out of icing.

"Just a little thing I baked up," said the beautiful Sabina modestly.

"All from a tin of sardines?" asked Tom suspiciously.

"Oh well, I've learned how to mix things and fix things," said the beautiful Sabina.

"It looks like a wedding cake," Tom remarked.

"So it does," cried Sabina in surprise. "I was trying to remember what it looked like."

"And," Tom went on boldly, "it seems a pity, having a wedding cake in the house, to waste it."

"That's a poetical thought, Tom," said the beautiful Sabina, smiling at him with her purple eyes.

So Tom and the beautiful Sabina were married absolutely straight away.

The mayor and the councillors and the policeman came to the wedding. There were some strange old women in pointed hats, too, but everyone was too polite to ask who they were. Everyone just said very politely how well they looked.

"There's a good doctor in this town," the old women replied, giving sharp sideways glances. "We hope he stays here. We'll get very cross if he doesn't."

So Tom stayed in his house where the walls were covered in poems. All day he wrote poetry and each night he cured a few witches. He grew rich and was able to afford a proper doctor's car.

The beautiful Sabina helped him. She wore a nurse's cap when he was doctoring and corrected the spelling of his poetry when he was writing. Some children said they had seen her riding off on her broomstick to witch parties, but their elders only said, "So what?"

"It's not every doctor that things work out so well for," Tom said, "and not every poet either."

The beautiful Sabina smiled with her pink lips and her purple eyes.

And they lived happily ever after.

The Princess and
the Clown

"Why are they ringing the bells?"

"Don't you know? The Princess is marrying the clown today."

"A princess marrying a clown? Are you sure? Princesses don't marry clowns. They marry princes,

simpletons and seventh sons; they marry the youngest of three brothers, but not clowns."

"No, I am quite sure this princess is marrying a clown, a tumbling patchwork fellow with a painted smile who falls flat on his face when he bows. If someone stands on his toe, water squirts out of his hat. This might be embarrassing at a State ball where everyone's toes get trodden on, but the Princess is going to marry him just the same."

"Well, is this a *plain* princess?"

"No, she is beautiful, this Princess, a bit like a birthday cake and a bit like moonlight. She is warm and glowing like the birthday cake, and yet she is silvery like moonlight. She is like the first rocket going up, and spilling its stars on Guy Fawkes night—you know, when it is not quite dark and somebody can't wait so they set this first rocket off. It climbs so high it can see over the edge of the world and it calls to the sun, 'Look at me, brother!' Then it hesitates and opens up like a rose of flame, dropping petals of fire. That is the most magical rocket of all and the Princess is like that, or like the unicorn, rare and only. Anyhow, she is beautiful."

"Why is she marrying a clown then?"

"It's a long story because lots of princes, dazzling in gold and diamonds, came and asked her, 'Princess, will you marry me?' and a lot of wise men with clever answers came to ask the same question. Hundreds of youngest sons appeared from all walks of life and asked the Princess if she'd marry them, but she always said, 'Not today, thank you', to them all.

"This made them very angry and they got together and wondered how to pay her back for refusing to marry any of them.

"One day they went to her father, the King, and told him they had just the husband for her, and her father, the King, said, 'Righto—we'll see him at dinner then, when pudding's over, just before we have coffee.'

"The heralds all blew on their trumpets when the pudding plates were being carried away, and in came the clown. He did not even know he was supposed to be asking for the Princess. He thought he was there to dance his dances and to make people laugh. This was a trick of the suitors to tease the clown and mock the Princess. The clown bowed to the King and the Princess and began to dance. He danced like a piece of crumpled wastepaper in the wind, twirling high and pettering low, and everyone laughed at him except the

74

Princess who looked at him with grey eyes, gentle and calm.

"The clown trod on his own toe and water squirted out of the top of his hat. His smile was wide and painted on, and his red wig waved wildly in the air like a sort of lion's mane.

"He took out a little violin, the size of a toothbrush and began to play. Music as sweet as honeysuckle twined into the air, but as he played so beautifully his trousers slid down showing red striped underpants and knobbly knees. Everyone laughed and laughed but the Princess rested her chin on her hands and watched more closely. He danced his desolate little wastepaper dance again and played his violin while he spun and peeped, but people only laughed all the harder, for his coat split down the back and fell around him in coloured tatters like autumn rags. Then at last he bowed to the King, and as he did so he fell flat on his face—that clown.

"The King got to his feet. He was laughing and angry at the same time. 'You!' he shouted. 'How dare you ask to marry my daughter!'

"The clown looked amazed. He did not know what the jealous suitors had told the King.

"But the Princess got up from her chair. 'Dear Clown,' she said, 'I love you and will marry you if you like.'

"'In that coat?' asked someone.

"'In it or out of it,' said the Princess. 'At least life would never be dull with a clown in the family.'

"'Princess,' said the clown, 'you mustn't marry me. I make people laugh but I am not a cheerful person

75

to live with. I'm really pretty sad.' He took out a large
red handkerchief, quite as big as a dishcloth and wiped
off his paint and powder face. Off came his smile, his
black eyebrows, his scarlet cheeks. Off came his red
wig. The face of an ordinary man looked out at the
world—young, a bit scared, rather sad and quite usual.

"Everyone laughed all over again.

"'Well,' said the Princess, 'when I'm sad you can
make me laugh, and when you're sad I will try and
make you laugh. That's fair, isn't it—but mind you,
don't be cross with me if I'm not very good to begin
with, because princesses aren't meant to make people
laugh.'

"'Well, personally,' said the King, 'I'm glad she's made up her mind at last. You shall marry this fine clown, my dear, if that is what you want, and maybe I'll get a laugh or two between the two of you whenever I come to visit. A laugh or two would spice even your cooking, my dear.'

"The suitors did not even smile any more after that, but the King, who guessed their trick, laughed louder and louder.

"So the Princess is to marry the Clown and they will live part of the year in his caravan. Their lives will be grave and gay like night and day and they will parade like kings or dance like wastepaper—whatever they feel like—and probably live happily ever after.

"Let off all the fireworks, and blow up all the balloons, ring all the bells, blow all the trumpets . . . a princess is marrying a clown and they will have children half kings and queens, half tumble-down clowns, who will lead us through the twisted ways of the world with laughter."

The Great Tractor Rescue

Stories about children driving powerful and dangerous machines have always been favourites. A tractor may seem humble compared with some machines, but it is dangerous for children to try to drive one. So, wait until you are grown up, and meanwhile—enjoy this story.

There was once a pair of boys called Teddy and Gerard who lived in a long secret valley. Wherever they looked there were hills, dark spiky pine trees, and bright streams filled with eels and watercress. It was just the sort of valley for boys to enjoy themselves in. Each weekday they went to school, but Saturday and Sunday were all their own, and they wandered all over the valley visiting both friends and friendly places.

One of their friends was a very strange old woman indeed. Her name was Mrs Estelle Tadworthy and she had a son who was a bank manager and lived the respectable life. Mrs Estelle Tadworthy, however, was not respectable. Everyone called her Mrs Weeds, because every weekend she left her house in the town and came out to the country to collect plants. Not garden plants either, for she scorned those. She chose the wild and weedy ones. She did not ever call them weeds, however, but always referred to them as "herbs". Most people thought Mrs Weeds was a little mad and she did look rather unusual wearing curious brown smocks which she wove and dyed herself, and funny old sandals tied up with string. She wouldn't wear a hat at all. Her long grey hair either tossed and tangled around her brown face or stuck out in two tight little plaits with green ribbons on the end. Rain or shine she always carried a stout green umbrella. It didn't worry her when people said she was crazy.

"Because I'm brown doesn't mean I'm dirty," she would say. "Because I don't do the same as every other fool, but like my own foolishness best, doesn't mean to say I'm crazy. Some like me, some don't," said Mrs Weeds. "That's how it is. . . ."

Teddy and Gerard were two who liked her a lot. They liked her thin bony face and long gentle hands. They liked the way she roared with laughter at her own jokes, the way she wore purple clover flowers behind her ears and the way she talked to plants and trees as she went along the road. She gave the boys all sorts of leaves to eat, telling them how good they would be for them.

"This is sorrel and this is dandelion," she said. "Eat them both to help keep your livers clean." The boys found the dandelion leaves hot to taste, but they liked the tangy flavour of the sorrel. Mrs Weeds said her liver was extremely clean and that was why she never got headaches or grumpy feelings. "It's the dandelion and sorrel that does it," she said.

One Saturday, just before Christmas, when the foxgloves were out, ringing white and purple bells on every hillside in the valley, and when the streams and boggy bits were green and yellow with watercress and kingcups, Teddy and Gerard went crawling behind a hedge pretending to escape from enemies. There was a rich earthy smell because the farmer who owned the field was plough-

ing it up to plant turnips. In fact, the boys went past his
tractor standing alone by the gate where he had left it to go
home for lunch.

"Anyhow, I could drive that tractor," said Teddy.

"So could I," said Gerard, "but we haven't got time
now—our enemies will catch us if we wait to try out a
tractor." They went crawling on. Then suddenly they
heard a voice coming down the road. It was their friend
Mrs Weeds talking aloud to a particularly fine foxglove.

"Hello, you fellow in your purple coat!" she shouted
"It's a lovely day. Why are you leaning over like that? Do
you want to see who's going by or are your roots weak?"

"Shall we jump out and frighten Mrs Weeds?" asked Teddy in a whisper. Gerard thought perhaps Mrs Weeds would not like *that* at all, but while he was thinking this, someone else sprang out at Mrs Weeds from the other side of the road. Two tremendous tall fellows with guns and rope leaped out of the foxgloves and shouted.

"Hands up, Mrs Estelle Tadworthy!" (Which was Mrs Weeds' real name, you'll remember.) Mrs Weeds stopped and peered at them.

"You have the bleary-eyed look that shows a lack of Vitamin A. The humble carrot would help you a lot," she said sharply. "And who might you be?" It was plain, however, that they were wicked robbers or some such.

"We are thieves and bandits," said the uglier of the two men, pointing his gun at her. "I am the thief and he is the bandit. We are going to kidnap you and never ever let you go until your rich son, Mr John Tadworthy, prominent businessman and bank manager that he is, pays us £1,000 sterling."

"I'll pound you and I'll sterling your friend," Mrs Weeds replied, taking her umbrella in a firm grip. "The first one that comes near me shall taste the power of my strong right arm."

Which shows that, though people said Mrs Weeds was slightly mad, she was actually very sensible and brave as a lion. Gerard could see, however, that even brown strong Mrs Weeds couldn't fight two kidnappers with guns and a long snaky rope. Fortunately he had a plan. He whispered it to Teddy, and Teddy understood at once though it was very hard to hear, what with the defiant screams of Mrs Weeds and the yells of the robbers, who were being hit with the umbrella.

Gerard's plan was this—that Teddy should drive the farmer's tractor down the road to rescue Mrs Weeds. In the meantime, he, Gerard, the best runner in the school, would try to lead at least one of the kidnappers away so that there would be only one left for Mrs Weeds and Teddy to deal with. Once round the corner Gerard would climb up a certain tree, and it would be Teddy's job to drive the tractor and Mrs Weeds underneath that tree so that Gerard could drop down onto it from the branches like a monkey or Tarzan in the pictures. This way, said Gerard, they would have an exciting adventure and be helpful to Mrs Weeds as well.

Teddy could scarcely get at the tractor quickly enough. He made off, hidden by the hedge while Gerard crouched in the soft ploughed earth watching the battle that raged in the road. Mrs Weeds was fighting magnificently, but she was getting a bit tired. You could not expect an old woman to fight both a thief and a bandit even if she was a fine muscular old woman with a remarkably clean liver.

Teddy went straight to the farmer's tractor. Quick as a flash he tried the knobs and levers and found how to start it immediately. He steered it round and out through the gateway forgetting, in his hurry, to open the gate. Fortunately, its hinges were rusty and old and snapped easily, so Teddy was very soon grinding down the road,

with the tractor in top gear, off to rescue Mrs Weeds. The only troublesome thing was the gate which was stuck across the front of the tractor.

Now when Gerard heard the tractor grating along the road and knew Teddy was coming, he wriggled out under the hedge and shouted, "Leave Mrs Weeds alone!" He charged fiercely at the thief.

The thief was just about to pop a loop of rope over Mrs Weeds' head when Gerard butted him squarely in the stomach. "Oof!" said the thief and sat down hard on the road.

"I'm off to get the police," Gerard said. "I shall tell them who you are, and describe your pasty faces to the last miserable whisker."

Naturally the kidnappers could not allow that.

"You look after the old woman and I'll catch the boy. We'll kidnap them both," yelled the bandit, and set off after Gerard leaving the thief to struggle with Mrs Weeds. You could see the bandit did not know that Gerard was a splendid runner—the fastest in the school.

At this moment Teddy drove the tractor into sight, steering it straight for Mrs Weeds and the thief.

"Jump on, Mrs Weeds," he called. "Jump on!" And, looking up and seeing what was coming and who was driving it, Mrs Weeds thrust her knobbly right fist at the thief, in a fine upper-cut, and scooping up her umbrella from the road, skilfully ducked round the gate (which still hung in front of the tractor), and nipped up beside Teddy. The thief was rather dazed. First he had been butted by Gerard and then boxed by Mrs Weeds. But worse was in store for him. He was too bewildered to notice the gate. As he went to leap after Mrs Weeds he hit the gate and lay flattened and dusty while the tractor ground on its way.

"I shall hit his fingers with my umbrella if he tries to climb after us," said Mrs Weeds, but the thief just lay in the dust and let them go on, steadily but not very fast.

They went round the corner. There was the tree with the bandit standing underneath it, looking into the branches that reached out over the road. There among the leaves crouched Gerard, like a monkey boy. The bandit who did not like climbing trees was trying to poke him down with a stick. He stopped and peered through his horn-rimmed glasses in astonishment. He dodged out of the way of the sticking-out gate and tried to scramble onto the tractor to get at Teddy and Mrs Weeds. Mrs Weeds was waiting with her umbrella and he had to let go again. As the tractor passed under the tree Gerard swung down from the branches onto it. Off they went, leaving the bandit and the thief behind.

Mrs Weeds roared with delighted laughter, startling a bull in a nearby paddock.

"You're a fine couple of fellows," she said. "More than a match for any kidnappers. Usually I like a bit of a scrap, but I was getting out of breath, I must admit." She slapped them on their backs. Teddy and Gerard looked proudly at each other out of the corners of their eyes. They grinned at Mrs Weeds. The tractor went rumble rumble bumble along the road. All seemed happy.

But . . . just at that moment a car roared up behind them and sitting at the wheel, his eyes narrow and fierce behind his glasses, was the bandit, while at his side, looking bruised and angry, sat the thief.

"Of course! They would have a car hidden!" cried Teddy in despair, for the car went much faster than the tractor. "What shall we do?"

Then Mrs Weeds climbed up onto the engine of the

tractor and unscrewed the petrol cap. From the wide pockets of her smock she took dandelions, sorrel, yarrow, forgetmenots, wild parsley and mint, clover, nettles and all sorts of plants, jammed them into the tank and then screwed the cap on again. Teddy, looking over his shoulder, saw the thief leaning out of the car window and trying to lassoo the tractor with the rope he had been using earlier for tying up Mrs Weeds. But at that moment the tractor gave a roar like a bull and leaped forward at the speed of an express railway train. It was plain that Mrs Weeds' plants had mingled with the petrol in some mysterious way to make a powerful mixture that the tractor loved. Teddy steered, Gerard worked the gears, and Mrs Weeds stood, tall and brown, with her grey hair blowing out like a flag in the wind they made by going so fast.

"We've left them miles behind," said Gerard, turning round. But no! There behind them bumping and bowling along was the kidnappers' car, and the bandit and thief were crouched inside it white as unpleasant cheese, and obviously terrified. The lassoo the thief had thrown had first caught the tractor and then whipped itself into a knot round the car's bumper. Neither the bandit nor the thief could get out of the car and the car could not get free of the tractor, so they sped wildly along together, on and on up hill and down until they came in sight of the nearest town. The tractor dashed into the main street, and then suddenly, without warning, it slowed down, and it stopped right in front of the police station.

A policeman with a ginger moustache was standing outside. He looked first at the tractor and then peered into the car.

"My word!" he shouted. "Here are those wicked criminals—the bandit and the thief. Catch them, catch them!" He blew on his whistle and policemen of all shapes and sizes came running from everywhere, seized the white-faced and trembling bandit, the battered and bruised thief and hurried them into prison, which was where they belonged.

So that was the end of the great tractor rescue in which Teddy and Gerard rescued their friend Mrs Weeds from kidnappers. But it was not quite the end because next weekend, Mrs Weeds came out to visit them and brought with her boxes of delightful seeds with instructions on how to grow them. They dug and planted (and Mrs Weeds dug and planted with them) and then they waited—and sure enough, two weeks later up came sage, up came parsley, marjoram, thyme, sweet basil, summer savory, dill, and all the nice garden herbs (pot herbs, as some call them) that give good rich tastes and smells to cooking. The boys' mother was delighted and the boys themselves were proud to have such good herb gardens, and looked after them carefully.

As for Mrs Weeds, she went on roaming the country-side, and when the story of the great tractor rescue got round, no kidnapper ever dared approach her as she strode on her way, her hair blowing grey and wild around her, her stout green umbrella under her arm, talking to trees and flowers as if they were the best of friends, as indeed they were.

The Good Wizard
of the Forest

There was once a wizard who thought he was wicked. Everyone else thought he was wicked too, but he wasn't really. It was just that his magic used to go wrong.

He wasn't a very *good* wizard.

However, though he wasn't a good wizard, he was a remarkable cook. He made wonderful chocolate cakes with ten eggs beaten up in them and melted chocolate poured on top. He wanted to give a chocolate cake party and invite all the children in town. He sent out invitations for tea and chocolate cake on special party cards, but nobody came. The children thought he was wicked. They thought he would turn them into creepie-crawlies. They did not know he could make wonderful chocolate cakes, so they stayed at home.

He had no pets and no friends.

Then one day he found a seedling tree—a little scraggly apple tree trying to grow among some stones.

"A tree might be company," thought the wizard, "though trees don't really appreciate chocolate cake." He dug it up, took it home with him and planted it by his back door.

"But you needn't think I'm going to spoil you, just because I've adopted you," said the wizard severely. "I'm not going to waste a lot of time watering you and hoeing round you."

The tree wilted.

"Oh, all right!" snapped the wizard. "Just a bit of water then!"

He bought a special red watering-can, and sprinkled the hot summer earth beside the tree. The tree grew and stretched out green arms to the sun.

The wizard stared sadly over the summer fields, brown and gold, to the chimneys and roofs of the town.

"I wish someone would come and have morning tea with me," he said.

The tree rustled its new leaves. The wizard had an idea.

"Perhaps a smidgeon of plant food?" he said to it.

Just for fun he made a wonderful plant-food cake. He made it of leaf mould and compost, with a pinch of nitrogen. He frosted it with lime. Then he put it on a

beautiful plate, a plate with roses on it that he had won
in a raffle. He put this plate on his best tea tray with the
red watering-can full of water beside it, and carried it out
to the tree. After this, on his second-best tray, he put a
cup of tea and a big slice of chocolate cake.

The wizard and the tree had morning tea together
in the sunshine.

"Shall I pour?" asked the wizard politely. He
sprinkled the tree with water from the red watering-can.
Then he poured himself a cup of tea.

"Do try a slice of this cake," said the wizard. "I
made it only this morning." He gave the tree a slice of the
plant-food cake, crumbling it round the tree roots. Then
he took a mouthful of chocolate cake. "Oh, good . . .
chocolate cake! My favourite!" said the wizard, pretending it was a great surprise.

Ever after this, the wizard and the tree had morning

and afternoon tea together. When the wizard made himself a chocolate cake, he made a plant-food cake for the tree. It kept him busy, and he stopped being quite so lonely.

"I wonder if trees get lonely for other trees," the wizard pondered. "How about a bit of leafy company?"

He began collecting more trees and planting them round his door. This meant making more plant-food cakes. The wizard carried a slice to each tree every morning, but his very first tree, his apple tree, was the one he always sat with and talked to.

The trees grew taller and taller. The wizard's house came to be filled with green shadows and golden splish-splashes of sunlight. Through his dreams the rustling of leaves ran like whispered music.

Even when he woke up in the morning the music went on. When he walked or ran it was as if he moved in tune to the steps of a secret dance.

Time went by. The wizard planted more and more trees. Other wizards forgot him, and the witches did not invite him to their sprightly midnight Soup-and-Spell parties.

One day, after many years, this wizard was sitting under his great old apple tree eating chocolate cake.

"May I offer you a slice?" he said to it, polite as ever. "May I pour you a cup?"

He crumbled plant-food cake round its roots, and sprinkled it with water from his battered old red watering-can.

Suddenly voices came to his ears, voices like clear chattering water. Out through the trees came a group of children in bright summery clothes.

The wizard stared at them and thought he knew them.

"Is that you, Billy Borage?" he asked. "Is that you, Sorrell Silk?"

"Billy Borage was my grandfather," said the boy. "But I'm Billy too."

"Sorrell Silk was my great-aunt," said a little girl, "but I'm named after her."

"Are you the good Wizard of the Wood?" asked another child.

"*What* wood?" asked the wizard, puzzled.

"*This* wood, silly," said Sorrell gently.

The wizard stared round him. The brown and golden fields had all disappeared. Trees and trees and

trees grew strong and branching everywhere. He could not see the end of them.

"How time flies," he murmured softly to himself. He turned to the children.

"This isn't a wood!" he told them. "These are just my trees and I am a wicked wizard, not a good one."

A strange rustling sound swept through the forest.

"The trees are laughing!" cried the wizard, who knew by now when trees laughed, and also when they wept. "Have I planted a forest by accident? Have I turned into a good wizard without noticing? I don't feel bad, but then I never did."

"We found some old invitations in the town museum," said Billy. "They were in a drawer marked 'Very Dangerous', but the cards were so pretty we thought they could not be really wicked."

"Only a *good* wizard would bother to plant a forest," said Sorrell. "So we thought we'd come to see—to see——"

"—if you had any chocolate cake left," cried all the other children, laughing.

"There's always chocolate cake," said the wizard joyfully. "Climb up into the tree. Eat apples while you wait. I'll just cut the chocolate cake up into slices. Do you like small slices or big ones?"

"Big ones!" shouted all the children.

"That's funny!" said the wizard. "So do I."

The trees rustled and the children sang. The wizard cut his big chocolate cake into big slices. The party was happening at last. Trees were company for trees. People were company for people. Trees were company for people and people were company for trees.

Nobody was lonely.

And there was plenty of cake for everyone, everyone laughing and everyone leafy.

So *that* was all right.

Looking for a Ghost

Running along the footpath, fire in his feet, came Sammy Scarlet. He ran on his toes, leaping as he ran, so that he seemed to dance and spin through the twilight like a grey, tumbling bird learning to fly. Sammy leaped as he ran to keep himself brave. He was going to a haunted house. That evening he was going to see a ghost for the first time in his life.

The haunted house was along a city street. It was

the last house left in the street, falling to pieces in the middle of a garden of weeds. The glass in the windows was broken, and some of them were crossed over with boards. There was a tall fence round it, but in some places the fence was tumbling down.

"They'll put a bulldozer through that old place soon," said the man in the shop at the corner. "That's a valuable section, a commercial section."

"Haunted?" Sammy had asked.

"They say there's a ghost, but it only comes out in the evening after the shops have shut up and most people have gone home. I've never seen it," said the man in the corner shop, "and I'm not hanging around here after five-thirty just to watch some ghost. Only a little one too, they say."

"A twilight ghost," Sammy said to himself, and felt as if something breathed cold on the back of his neck, and whispered with cold lips in his ear.

Now he ran swiftly through the early evening. Sammy had chosen his time carefully . . . not so dark that his mother would worry about him, not too light for a small, cold ghost.

"Just a quick prowl around!" thought Sammy, as he ran and leaped to keep away the fear which ran beside him like a chilly, pale-eyed dog.

"If I go back now, I'm a coward," thought Sammy, and leaped again. "I've promised myself to see a ghost and I'm *going* to see a ghost."

He knew the street well, but evening changed it. It took him by surprise, seeming to have grown longer and emptier. And at the end of the street the haunted house was waiting. Sammy could see its gate and its tired tumbledown fence. By the gate something moved softly. Sammy leaped in his running, matching his jump to the jump of his heart. But the shadow by the gate was only a little girl bouncing a ball with a stick. She looked up as Sammy came running towards her.

"Hello," she said. "I thought no one ever came here in the evening."

"I've come," Sammy answered, panting. "I'm going to see the ghost."

The little girl looked at him with shadowy black eyes. "A real ghost?" she asked. "What ghost?"

"A ghost that haunts this house," Sammy replied. He was glad of someone to talk to, even a girl with a striped rubber ball in one hand and a stick in the other. She looked back at the house.

"Is this house haunted?" she asked again. "I suppose it looks a bit haunted. It's got cobwebs on it, and thistles in the garden. Aren't you frightened of the ghost, then?"

"I'm not scared of ghosts," said Sammy cheerfully. (He hoped it sounded cheerful.) "They can be pretty scary to some people but, I don't know how it is, somehow they don't scare me. I'm going through the fence to take a look. They say it is only a little one."

"Why don't you try the gate?" suggested the girl, pushing at the gate with her stick. It creaked open. Sammy stared.

"That's funny," he said. "I looked at the gate earlier and it was locked."

"I'll come with you," said the girl. "My name is Belinda, and I would like to see a ghost too."

"I don't think you'd better," replied Sammy,

frowning, "because ghosts can be pretty horrible, you know . . . with sharp teeth and claws and cackling laughs. Bony too!"

"There's nothing wrong with being bony," said Belinda.

She was very thin with a pale, serious face and long brown hair. Though she did not smile she looked friendly and interested. Her heavy shoes made her legs look even thinner, and her dress was too big for her, Sammy thought. Certainly it was too long, giving her an old-fashioned look.

"If it's scary to be bony," said Belinda, "I might frighten the ghost. Anyway the gate is open and I can go in if I want to." She stepped into the old garden and Sammy stepped after her, half cross because she was coming into his private adventure, half pleased to have company. As he came through the gate Sammy felt a cold breath fall on the back of his neck. Turning round slowly he saw nothing. Perhaps it was just a little cool wind sliding into the empty garden with them.

"A garden of thistledown and dandelions," Belinda cried. "A garden all for birds and beetles and ghosts." She seemed to like what she saw. "The lawn is almost as tall as my shoulder. A ghost could easily be in that long grass, and just rise up beside us like smoke."

Sammy glanced thoughtfully at the grass, half expecting a smoky shape to billow up and wave its arms at him. But—no smoke, no sound. It was all very still. He could hear cars out on the main road, but they seemed like thin dreams of sound, tiny flies buzzing far away. He walked up the brick path and stood on the front steps of the haunted house, looking at its sad

veranda. One of the carved posts was crumbling down and the veranda sagged with it.

"You'd feel cruel just standing on this veranda," Sammy remarked. "It looks so limp and sick."

"Cruelty to verandas!" said Belinda seriously. "Stand on it lightly, Sammy, and we'll go inside. I think a ghost would be more likely to be inside, don't you?"

"The door will be locked, won't it?" Sammy said. Then, "How did you know my name?" he asked, looking puzzled.

"You *look* like a Sammy," was all she said. She pushed the door and it slowly opened, like a black mouth opening to suck them into its shadows.

"I might stay out here," Sammy said. "The floor could cave in or something." His voice was quiet and squashed small by the heavy silence of the whole house and garden.

"You don't have to be afraid," Belinda told him kindly. "It's just an old, empty house, and old houses were made of good wood." Through the dark door she slid and vanished. Sammy *had* to follow her. Then he got the most terrible fright. He was standing in a hall so dim and dusty that he could see almost nothing. But what he *could* see was a dim and dusty figure at the other end of the hall moving slowly towards him.

"The ghost!" cried Sammy.

Belinda looked back at him. He could not see her face properly, but for some reason he thought she might be smiling.

"It isn't a ghost," she told him. "It's a looking-glass. There's a tall cupboard at the end with a look-

100

ing-glass in its door. It's your own reflection that's frightening you."

Sammy blinked and saw that what she said could be true. They walked cautiously up the hall. The looking-glass reflected the open doorway behind them. It was so dark inside that the evening outside looked bright and pearly.

Sammy rubbed his finger across the looking-glass.

The looking-glass moved and they heard a low moaning.

"The ghost!" gasped Sammy again, but it was just the cupboard door. It was a little bit open, and creaking when Sammy touched it.

"Come upstairs!" Belinda said. "They were nice, once, these stairs. They used to be polished every day."

"How can you tell?" asked Sammy, looking up the dark stairway.

"They are smooth under the dust," Belinda replied, "smooth with feet walking, and hands polishing. But that was a long time ago."

"How can you see your way upstairs?" Sammy asked. "It's so dark."

"There's enough light," she answered, already several steps above him. Sammy came after her. Out of the dark came a hand, soft and silent as the shadows, and laid silken fingers across his face.

"The ghost!" cried Sammy for the third time.

"Cobwebs, only cobwebs!" called Belinda back to him. Sammy touched his face. His own fingers, stiff with fright, found only cobwebs, just as Belinda had said. He stumbled and scrambled up after her onto the landing. There was a window boarded over. It was easy to peep through the cracks and look over the thistly garden and down the empty street.

"There used to be grass there," Belinda whispered, peering out. "Grass and cows. But that was a long time ago." She straightened up. "Come through *this* door," she said in her ordinary voice.

Sammy did not want to be left behind. They went through the door into a small room. The boards had partly slipped away from the windows. Evening light brightened the walls and striped the ceiling. There were the remains of green curtains and a rocking-chair with one rocker broken. Sitting in the chair was a very old doll. It looked as if someone had put it down and had gone out to play for a moment. The doll seemed to expect someone to be back to play with it. Sammy looked over to the doll and around the room, and then out through the window. "There's no ghost," he said, "and it's getting late. I'll have to be going."

The ghost did not seem as important as it had a moment ago, but Sammy thought he would remember the silent, tumbling house and its wild garden, long after he had stopped thinking about ghosts.

They went down the stairs again and Sammy did not jump at the cobwebs. They went past the looking-glass and he creaked the cupboard door on purpose this time. Now the sound did not frighten him. It was gentle and complaining, not fierce or angry.

"It only wants to be left alone," Belinda said, and that was what it sounded like.

They walked down the hall and Sammy turned to wave goodbye to his reflection before he shut the door.

The reflection waved back at him from the end of a long tunnel of shadow. Outside, the evening darkened. Stars were showing.

"No ghost!" said Sammy, shaking his head.

They walked to the gate.

"Will you be coming back some other night to look for the ghost?" Belinda asked.

"I don't think so," Sammy answered. "I don't really believe in ghosts. I just thought there might be one. I've looked once and there isn't one and that's enough."

He turned to run off home, but something made him stop and look sharply at Belinda.

"Did you see *your* reflection in that looking-glass?" he asked curiously. "I don't remember your reflection.'

Belinda did not answer his question. Instead she asked him one of her own.

"Everyone has a reflection, don't they?" It was hard to see her in the late evening, but once again Sammy thought she might be smiling.

"You went up the stairs first," he went on. "Why didn't you brush the cobwebs away?'

"I'm not as tall as you," Belinda said.

Sammy peered at her, waiting for her to say something more. Just for a moment, very faintly, he felt that chilly breeze touch the back of his neck again.

"No ghost!" he said at last. "No such things as ghosts!" Then, without a goodbye, he ran off home, rockets in the heels of his shoes.

Belinda watched him go.

"The question is," she said to herself, "whether he would recognize a ghost, supposing he saw one."

She went back through the gate and locked it carefully after her. She was already faint and far off in the evening, and as she pushed the bolt home she disappeared entirely.

The Green Fair

Look, children, look at the fair.

It has come in the night. It is there.

Like a flock of bright birds the tents have settled, spreading their wings in the morning wind.

There are two merry-go-rounds waiting. There is popcorn, candy floss, fizzy lemonade and ice cream. There are tents with wonderful things inside them— ghost trains, mermaids, merry monkeys, clever mice that can dance a jig and play on drums no bigger than walnuts.

The farmers have brought all their animals to win prizes—horses stamp, cows moo. The sheep blink sadly at each other. The pigs snuffle and sleep.

The fair is waiting to begin. All over town people

open doors. The children spill outside, laughing and shouting in the clear morning sunlight.

On the edge of the fair is a little brown tent; it is like a pine cone in the grass.

Who is it sitting outside the little tent? His thin hands on his knees are like rustly brown leaves curled around each other.

At the doorways of the other gay tents men shout and dance and call people in. This man does not smile or shout. He is as still as a man carved of wood.

Only the magpies and the sparrows come to his tent and he lets them inside. What is inside the brown tent, the pine-cone tent small and still on the edge of the noisy fair?

Two big boys come by. They have jingly money in their pockets.

"What's in this tent?" they ask the man outside.

"The Green Fair," says the man, and he looks at them with narrow green eyes, like blades of grass.

The Green Fair? What is the Green Fair?

"How much does it cost to go in?" the boys ask.

"It costs a silver piece to go inside."

"It is the cheapest tent in the whole show."

"It is too cheap and small to be any good," the boys say to each other. "We will have another ride on the merry-go-round."

Off they go, jingling their pockets.

"The Green Fair?" says a woodmouse who is listening. "What is the Green Fair?"

"It is free to mice," says the man. The mouse scurries into the little brown tent, the pine-cone tent, on the edge of the fair.

Then a lot of little children come by. The oldest is seven and the smallest is three. They have no money. They are looking for bottles to sell.

"What is in this tent?" they ask the man.

"The Green Fair," he says. He smiles for the first time.

"Why don't you stamp and shout? Why don't you call people in?" asks a little girl.

"I don't need to," says the man. "The right people come to me. It costs a silver piece to go in."

"We don't even have a silver piece," says a boy.

"What is that by your foot?" asks the man. There by the boy's foot a silver piece lies in the grass. Perhaps one of the big boys dropped it.

"We can buy popcorn now," cried a child. But no—all the children want to go into the little brown pine-cone tent. They all want to see the Green Fair.

"Everybody can go in for a silver piece," says the man. "Here are your tickets."

What is this? He gathers a handful of grass. Each child takes a blade of grass and goes into the little brown tent. It is so small they have to get down on their knees to go in.

Inside the tent . . . what is inside the tent?

A forest of tall trees.

Perhaps it is the oldest forest of all. Perhaps it has been growing there since the first morning. Moss has spread out over the trunks and branches.

How can an old old forest be growing in a little brown tent?

How can the trees be so tall and stretch so wide?

"Is it magic?" asks a child.

"Magic," says an echo, as if the forest was answering, but really the forest is still, so still you can hear the spiders spin their cobwebs. The children think it must be magic. The forest feels magical—it is quiet waiting for something to happen.

Under the trees is a merry-go-round. Its horses swing on ropes plaited of rushes and its roof is covered with ferns and moss.

Perhaps it is the oldest merry-go-round in the world.

Perhaps someone planted a seed there—a merry-go-round seed—which grew into a merry-go-round.

There are just enough horses for the children to have one each. They scramble on, the horses begin to toss their heads and kick up their heels. Slowly they begin their dance round and round in the green light of the forest.

108

Look—the forest comes alive. Out from under the ferns come little animals carrying wooden dishes of fruit—the plum, the pear, the apple, and grapes both white and purple. Someone begins to play on a penny whistle.

The Green Fair has begun.

Now the furry people put up small green stalls. They smile all over their whiskery faces and beckon the children to come and see. Everything in the Green Fair is free. You can win prizes too.

You can win—a nest of singing birds,

> a bear carved out of a cherry stone,
> a doll tiny enough to live in a matchbox,
> a tiger skin with fierce eyes and white teeth,
> a pair of dancing shoes sewn all over with flowers,
> a cricket in a cage of willow.

Every child wins a prize, even the smallest child of all. She wins a little wooden box. When she opens the box a frog plays a tune on a green fiddle. She must remember to give the frog brown bread soaked in milk, or he will hop away. Yes, he will hop away and take his green fiddle with him.

All the time the merry-go-round goes round and round, round and round, under the green leaves.

The bush rats come out from the mossy hollows. They are the music-makers. They play on the drum, the flute, the bells and the tinkle-tankle harp.

The children can listen and laugh, they can dance and sing. They don't need to know any words. They can make them up.

"Oh, the Green Fair!
Oh, the Green Fair!
And everyone happy under the leaves."

110

Now the feasting begins.
Out come dishes of nuts,
    plates of little cakes,
    shivery jellies coloured like rainbows,
    leaves filled with blackberries,
    flowers filled with strawberries,
    honey from a wild bee's nest, dripping golden
    from the honeycomb.
    There is a fire. You can sizzle sausages if you want
to. You wrap them in a slice of fresh brown bread and
eat them hot, hot, hot. They are burnt on the outside,
but that is all the better.
    There is fizzy lemonade. As you open the bottle

it sings its song to you. There is grape juice and apple juice and slices of orange.

This is the feast of the Green Fair.

But the merry-go-round spins slower and slower. At last it stops. It is time to go. The Green Fair is over. The furry people fold up their stalls. The forest goes still again . . . so still you can hear the spiders spin their webs.

The children must go now, but they are happy, sticky children. (This is how children are when they have visited the Green Fair.) They hold their prizes tightly. They will keep them for ever. Their pockets are filled with the cakes and nuts they cannot eat. They whistle and sing and shout as they tumble home.

"Did you have a good time?" asks the mother of the littlest girl.

The littlest girl opens her wooden box. Up jumps the frog and plays a tune on his green fiddle.

"I must remember to give him bread and milk," she says, "and then he will stay for ever."

"Ah," says her mother, "you have been to the Green Fair. I went once when I was little like you. I

won a musical box, small as a bird's egg. I still have it in my box of treasures. It plays the songs of the Green Fair."

Late at night the big, bright fair is dark and still. The moon comes up. It sees a lonely light on the edge of the big fair. There sits the man beside his little brown tent.

His thin hands are like rustly brown leaves curled around each other. His narrow eyes shine like blades of grass in the moonlight. He lets the mice, the bush bats, the owls, the moths and the people of the night go into his tent.

They all want to visit the Green Fair.

As he sits there he remembers the littlest girl. He thinks of a long time ago, and remembers her mother. He remembers back to the oldest time of all when the old forest was planted and the Green Fair began to grow.

"The right people always find me," he thinks and he smiles.

The Bird Child

A certain small girl once lived in a big city which had a forest on its northern edge and an orphanage on its southern edge. The little girl was an orphan herself. She had no father or mother, only an aunt. But this aunt was of the forgetful kind. One day, when they were having a picnic in the forest, the aunt forgot she had a little girl to look after. She wandered off home, packed her suitcase and went to South America. She was never heard of again.

The little girl waited and waited for her to come back. Fortunately the aunt had left her under a wild apple tree. She lay on her back watching the pattern of blue sky, green leaves and red apples. When the apples fell down she ate them. On the third day of waiting, two pigeons flew down and looked at the little girl very hard.

"Are you going to live here for ever?" they asked her, but the little girl was too small to explain that she had been left there by her aunt.

"My dear," said the father pigeon to the mother pigeon, "I think she has been left behind by some picnickers. They are always leaving eggshells and banana peel around. Now they have left a child."

"It is very untidy of them," said the mother pigeon. "Poor little girl! Shall we adopt her?"

Now, in this forest lived all the different kinds of birds in the world, and the pigeons called them all together. They began to make a special nest for the little girl. First of all they wove tree twigs together to make a floor and walls. Then the thrushes and blackbirds lined it with straw and mud to keep out the wind and rain. Then the sparrows, finches and warblers lined it with moss and feathers for softness.

Working together, some of the strongest birds lifted the little girl into the nest. They brought her black-berries and grass seed to eat, and even a few worms. She just opened her mouth and they poked food into it.

It was much easier than living with the aunt who used to say, "Sit up straight and don't make a lot of crumbs when you eat."

As the weeks went by, the birds grew very fond of

the little girl, and were always trying to think of ways to amuse her. Because she hated to see them fly away and leave her, they made her a pair of wings out of twigs and tree-gum and feathers. The little girl soon learned to use them cleverly. She flew with the birds in the sunshine. She soared and twisted in and out of the forest trees, chasing the birds and gathering her own blackberries and worms. Living like this she grew strong and brown and wild. Her hair was tangly, all full of leaves and flowers. Her clothes got torn to pieces and fell off, but this made it much simpler when she wanted to go swimming.

Every few months the birds made her a new pair of wings, brighter and stronger than those she had outgrown.

One day a hunter, hunting around, saw a flash of blue in the green trees. Flying on wings made by peacocks and kingfishers, the little girl spun into sight for a moment and then was lost again. The huntsman did not know that the birds had made her wings for her. He thought she had grown them all on her own. He went and brought back another hunter and a circus man. They set up a table in the middle of the forest with a birthday cake on it. Before long the Bird Child came down to look at it, and then the hunters threw nets over her. Her great wings broke and crumpled.

The hunters and the circus man were very angry when they found her wings were just tied on with ribbons woven of grass, but there was nothing they could do about it. So the hunters took the little girl out of the forest, right across the city to the orphanage. It was a square brown building in a square brown yard. The

116

woman in charge was Mrs Parsley. She did not enjoy her
job very much. She really wanted to spend her time
growing tomatoes and strawberries. Instead, she had to
look after thirty lively, grubby children. When the
hunters gave her the Bird Child she was not pleased.

"Tisk! Tsk!" she went with her tongue and took the
Bird Child inside. She scrubbed her and rubbed her but
she could not make her pale like the other orphans. She
could not brush her tangly hair either, so she snipped it
off. She dressed the Bird Child in a brown dress and put
shoes on her feet, so that she could not run. The walls
round the orphanage were tall as trees and there was a
lock on the gate.

The little Bird Child grew thinner and quieter. She

became paler than any of the other orphans. Mrs Parsley gave her cod-liver oil, but it did not make her better. (Mrs Parsley should have given her a beakful of honey or a few worms. But Mrs Parsley did not think of that.)

Once a week the Mayor of the city used to come and count the orphans. He was very proud of his neat, well-run orphanage.

"Where did the new orphan come from?" asked the Mayor. "She doesn't look to be a very good one."

"Some hunters found her in the forest," said Mrs Parsley. "You just don't know *where* orphans are going to turn up these days."

Just then the Mayor and Mrs Parsley heard a noise like the wind, though there was no wind. They looked up at the hills on the other side of the city and saw a cloud

rise from the secret heart of the forest. It swirled and eddied like smoke, but it was not smoke. It shimmered and shivered like silk, but it was not silk. Mrs Parsley and the Mayor stared uneasily. The cloud came closer.

"It's birds" said Mrs Parsley, amazed.

"Birds!" cried the Mayor like an echo.

Sparrows, thrushes, blackbirds, peacocks, pigeons, parrots and pelicans, firebirds, pheasants and flamingos, swans and seagulls, egrets and eagles, herons, humming-birds and various finches, all were flying straight towards the orphanage, making the air whisper and the leaves stir and rustle with the wind of their wings.

119

"Well, I've never seen so many birds!" said Mrs Parsley suspiciously. "It's not natural. They'll drop feathers all over the orphanage ground. And it's just been rolled and swept."

Down in the orphanage yard, one orphan looked up at the birds and cried out to them in a voice that was curious and lonely. She held up her arms as if she might fly up and join them. The cloud of birds wheeled and swept down, making a great storm. For a moment the Mayor and Mrs Parsley could see nothing but bright whirling feathers. Then the birds rose again and flew off towards the forest. They took all the orphans with them.

Mrs Parsley and the Mayor stared after them.

"Those birds have taken the Civic Orphans!" cried the Mayor. "And they haven't filled in any adoption forms."

The birds flew back to the forest. They had come to the orphanage looking for their Bird Child, but, because they could not tell one orphan from another, they had taken the lot. They carried all the orphans into the green shade of the forest, and began looking after them. First they built them nests, then they fed them with honey. The orphans sat in a row and the birds dropped honey into their open mouths. Then the birds made the orphans wings. All the orphans became Bird Children.

Mrs Parsley spent all that spring with a spade digging up the orphanage lawn. She grew the most remarkable tomatoes. On summer evenings she would look up from her garden to see the Bird Children, tossing like bright kites over the green roof of the forest, their wings wide and shining carrying them up towards the stars.

Green Needles

All round Teddy's house marched the pine trees—more than a hundred of them. Although they were so tall, and Teddy was so small they often nodded to each other, and Teddy felt very friendly towards them. He liked their grey, wrinkled skins and arms full of cones. He enjoyed the music the wind made in them, roaring like the sea.

One night, one of the trees fell with a crash like thunder and the end of the world. Now Teddy had a wonderful new playground as he climbed up and down and round about the fallen giant. He rode the springy branches as if they were wild, tossing horses and then slid down into pine-scented shadows below. The tree became Teddy's house, all little green rooms and passages.

Then one day while he was playing in his house he pushed through a curtain of needles and found himself in a room he had never seen before. Someone else was there before him.

"Hello!" said Teddy.

"Hello!" said the someone else.

They liked each other straight away. The someone else had greyish hair, and a brown, crinkled-up face. He wore a jacket and trousers made out of pine needles, and his eyes were green too, as green and sharp as the pine needles themselves.

"Are you a pine-tree man?" asked Teddy.

"Well, I live here at present," the man answered. "It suits me because my name actually is Green Needles and we

121

match, this tree and I. I am hiding from someone, so I have to match the place I hide in."

"Who are you hiding from?" Teddy asked.

"A very rich, powerful queen!" Green Needles said. "She is a bit too rich really. I did some work for her once and she wanted to keep me for forever. But no one can keep me for forever, because I don't care to be kept. Mine is a wild, free nature."

"What was the work you did?" Teddy wondered.

"It was sewing," Green Needles replied. Teddy thought he must mean "sowing" like sowing seeds in a garden, but Green Needles said he meant sewing with stitches and a needle.

"I can thread a needle with sunshine and sew gold, or with moonlight and sew silver. I can make my stitches with moss, or cobwebs, with the dust on fern fronds and the feathers of a kingfisher," boasted Green Needles, "but I must be free. So will you let me sit here in this green room and hide, until I am quite sure it is safe for me to go out in the world again? Sooner or later they will come and search for me here, and if they don't find me they will go away and never come back. I will be safe then. Will you hide me?"

"Of course I will," Teddy agreed, wondering who would come looking for Green Needles, "and I will visit you sometimes."

So that was what happened, and for several weeks Green Needles sat in his pine-tree room, while Teddy visited him and told him about the world. Then one day Teddy's mother said to him, "I am going to visit Mrs Shaw and I'm taking the babies. Can you be a good boy and look after the house while I am away? I won't be long." And off she went.

122

Teddy sat in the kitchen eating a bread slice with dates on it when the door opened. It wasn't his mother at all. It was three strange people with long, solemn faces. One was a soldier, tall and glittering in armour like fish scales. His black hair was braided with red ribbon, and in his hand he carried a long, slender spear. At his side swung a sword in a golden sheath. The second of the visitors was a woman tall and strong as a man, wearing a helmet crested with plumes and cloak of tiger skin over her armour. Her hair, bright as a flame, fell down over the cloak to her waist and twisted in it were chains of silver, and of roses. On her shoulder sat the third person, a little old, old man, so old he had shrunken back to child size. He was quite white. There was white in his clothes, in his face and in his hair. Only his eyes were black, and in his hand he clasped a little black wand, which he pointed at Teddy.

"You!" he cried. "You, little boy! My wand tells me Green Needles has been here. Where is he?"

"He isn't here," Teddy answered quite truthfully, because Green Needles was nowhere near the house.

"A queen wants him," the old, old man went on, "a powerful queen. She will give you boxes of pearls and yards of crimson silk, she will give you the furs of wild white foxes. Where is Green Needles?"

"I don't know!" Teddy shook his head, and this time it was a little lie, because he knew quite well Green Needles was sitting out in his secret piny room.

"The Queen will give more," declared the old man frowning at Teddy. "She will give fifteen baskets of scarlet roses and a musical box that sings like a blackbird. She will give a casket of silver lined with black velvet, holding a perfect diamond, and a casket of gold holding a single dew drop, also a singing cricket in a cage of ivory."

123

"I would like a cricket," Teddy said, "but I don't know where Green Needles is."

"Lastly," said the old man, looking furious, "the Queen will give to the boy who tells her where Green Needles is — a chair of gold by her own chair at the table. That boy will walk beside her in the great parades, or ride beside her on a pony white as snow, or sit beside her in her coach on a seat of midnight blue velvet, and be in all ways like a son to her."

"Well," Teddy shook his head, "I don't know at all where Green Needles is."

"My wand tells me you are lying," the old man said.

"Your wand needs fixing," Teddy said firmly in answer. Then the old man said angrily to his friends, "Search the house!"

They pushed past Teddy and marched into the kitchen. They pulled open the cupboards and flung the saucepans and the papers, the knives, the forks, the Mar-

mite, the butter and the good wholesome bread onto the floor. The soldier even poked the bag puddings with his spear. They went through the house, slashing and searching. They tore books and the sitting-room carpet. The huge woman pulled the curtains down, and tugged the drawers out of the desk. The soldier ripped the blankets off the beds, and sliced the mattresses in two. Oh, it was dreadful to see how they searched—how they slit and split, chipped and chopped, hashed and gashed, wrenched, splintered, carved and quartered, and tore to tatters the poor, old house. But they could not find Green Needles.

Then they went round and round the house, and even searched the pine tree, but they did not find Green Needles in his little secret room in the pine tree's heart. So at last they stopped.

"He isn't here!" said the large woman. "The magician's wand is wrong."

"My wand has never been wrong before," the old magician replied sulkily.

"This time it is wrong," the soldier grunted heavily, "or else Green Needles has a stronger magic than you."

"That miserable stitcher has no magic at all!" screamed the enraged magician. None of them took any notice of Teddy who was standing near by listening.

"Then your wand is wrong," the soldier sighed, "and we are wasting our time. Let us go and search some other world."

And they went off down the road, leaving Teddy to explain about the ruined house to his mother who was just coming down the hill.

Teddy's mother was not at all pleased. She could not be cross with Teddy for so nobly and bravely helping his friend, Green Needles, but it was plain she wanted to be.

126

"Look at the place!" she cried, over and over again. "Just look at it! What will your father say? He's bringing visitors home this evening, too. Look, they've even emptied out the vases. Oh, and the *inkwell*! They can't have thought your friend was hiding there."

But at that moment who should come in but Green Needles himself.

Teddy was amazed.

"You must hide!" he told Green Needles. "People are looking for you."

"Actually," Green Needles answered calmly, "I don't think they will come back. And so I can go on with my wanderings. I feel free again."

"I thought they would find you," Teddy said.

"Ah, but I sewed myself safely into the pine-tree room and they went by me a thousand times, not guessing I was there. So you see I am safe, and soon I will be on my way. But first, madam," with a bow to Teddy's mother, "I must help you."

"What can you do?" Teddy's mother asked, looking at the wreckage.

"Madam, I can sew!" said Green Needles. And he turned back his coat collar to show a row of green needles, some as thick as a big darning needle, others as fine as the feeler of an ant. From his pocket he took silks as many-coloured as summer time.

Yes, Green Needles could sew like nobody ever sewed before. He sewed up the tears in the wall with butterflies and birds. He sewed up the tears in the carpet and, where his needle flashed, primroses appeared, with hyacinths, jonquils, crocuses and the starry yarrow—all so real they seemed to nod in the wind. Teddy's mother didn't have a carpet any more. She had a garden in every room, a garden

127

you could walk over without bruising leaf or flower. The silks Green Needles sewed with smelled of rosemary and lavender and of pine trees.

Where the curtains had been slashed, Green Needles mended them. Some he sewed with ivy, and among the leaves he put birds' nests with blue eggs in them. Thrushes and blackbirds peeped out into the room. Other curtains he sewed with spiders' webs, fine and silken, and with dragon-flies and flag irises. He sewed the chairs with a mellow thread that looked like the rich shine in fine, polished wood.

Then he looked at the ceiling where the soldier's spear had poked and scarred.

"Now I shall thread my needle with sunshine," said Green Needles. He embroidered a laughing, jolly sun, and a silver secret moon in the centre of the ceiling, and round the edges he put the stars dancing in their beautiful patterns . . . the Ram, the Twins, Taurus the Bull, Capricorn the Goat, striding Orion and the shy Seven Sisters—all the starry people shone over Teddy's head.

Then he sewed up the mattresses with stitches like a procession of ladybirds. Even the pages of the books he stitched together with tiny white and black threads, so that you couldn't tell where they had been torn. Oh, Green Needles, Green Needles, there was never another like you —you were the greatest stitcher in the world.

Then Green Needles put his needles back in his coat collar, and his silks back in his pocket.

"Now I can be on my way," he said, "for they won't come here any more. They won't dare to admit I was hiding all the time and they missed me. If you knew what their Queen was like, you would understand. A handsome woman, mind you, but sharp in the temper. They've gone off to search for me among the stars."

128

"Are you sure you won't stay a little longer?" asked Teddy's mother. "Stay for tea!"

"I don't think so," said Green Needles. "My inside tells me I need space and sunshine, the open road and trees and flowers, stars and seas. In short, I need some wandering. The world gives me its colours, and its shapes and its shadows, and they all come out in my sewing. That is how I give them back to the world."

So they thanked him and off he went, and Teddy never saw him again in all the world. But the flowery carpets, the sun and the stars on the ceiling, the butterflies and kingfishers on the walls—these remained as if the outside world had come into Teddy's house to keep him company, and liked it so much it had decided to stay there. So after that, because he had helped Green Needles, Teddy walked sweet and saw gay, inside as well as out, for almost forever.

The Witch Dog

There was once a mother whose children had all grown up and gone working or got married. This mother now had nothing to do but tidy her already tidy house and weed her neat garden. This was not so very interesting for her. So, one day, this mother—her name was Mrs Rose—said to her husband, "Dear, I find life a bit slow just now, with the children all away. I think I'll join a club, or take a class in something."

"That's a good idea," said Mr Rose. "How about playing bowls?" (He played bowls himself, you see.)

"Well, no, I don't fancy that," said Mrs Rose. "I'd never be good enough to play with *you*, dear. No, I've had something in mind for a day or two: I think I'll learn to be a witch. I saw in the paper that they were having classes at night school."

"They certainly have some interesting classes at night school these days," said Mr Rose. "Just as you like, my dear. You will enjoy it."

Mrs Rose turned out to be very good at witchcraft. When other pupils were struggling to pull rabbits out of hats, Mrs Rose was able to pull out ribbons, sparrows, buttercups and daisies, little silver fish, frogs, dragonflies and poems written in gold on pink paper. She found it easy. The Head Witch was pleased.

"My dear Witch Rose," she said, "you are doing
excellently—EXCELLENTLY. You may come and dance
at our Witch Dance as soon as you have mastered your
broomstick technique." Mrs Rose was delighted—it was
a special honour to be allowed to dance in a witch dance,
and she knew she was the only one in the class to be invited.
She worked hard with her broomstick. First she learned to
balance and then to soar, and soon she was soaring and
swooping like a cinder in the wind.

"Well, Witch Rose," said the Head Witch, "you're a
most creditable pupil. Next Friday you may come to our

Witch Dance and we'll be pleased to have you. You must make yourself a cloak and hat and get yourself a cat, too, if you haven't got one already."

Mrs Rose suddenly looked very dismayed.

"A cat!" she said, but the Head Witch had whisked off hastily to talk to some other pupil not nearly as clever as Mrs Rose.

"A cat!" muttered Mrs Rose, for there was something she hadn't told the Head Witch—something she hadn't even thought about, something that meant perhaps, that she could never ever be a true witch and dance at the Witch Dances.

"How am I going to get along?" she cried to Mr Rose. "Cat's fur makes me sneeze my head off if the cat comes close. I won't be able to go, and I would like to, having got so far. But even a kitten makes me sneeze."

"Get a dog instead," said Mr Rose. "A small portable dog—one that will fit onto the end of a broomstick. I know it's not usual, but there we are—and dogs don't make you sneeze."

"Oh, do you think a dog would do instead?" Mrs Rose said. "I wonder. . . . That's a good idea of yours, Tom. I'll think about it." She didn't have to think long, for by a curious coincidence the first thing she saw when she went out for the milk next morning was a funny little lost dog—just the sort that could fit on the end of a broomstick. He had no collar but had a cheerful expression and Mrs Rose liked him at once. She liked his silvery grey coat, which was shaggy and hung down almost to his feet, and she liked his merry ears which stuck up straight into the air and then changed their minds and hung down at the tips.

"Would you like to be a witch dog?" Mrs Rose asked

133

him, and he wriggled his nose in a dog-grin and wagged his tail. "Very well," said Mrs Rose, "you shall be, and I will call you 'Nightshade'. That's a good witch name, and ought to please the witches."

On Saturday night Mrs Rose put on her hat and cloak and tucked her wand into her belt. She climbed onto her broomstick. Nightshade hopped on behind as if he had been born to it. A moment later they were up in the air and Mrs Rose pointed her broomstick in the direction of Miller's Hill.

Already the bare place at the top of Miller's Hill was bustling and rustling with witches—lots of witches. They had lighted a huge fire and were standing around it, some with cats and some with solemn owls. When Mrs Rose and Nightshade glided down amongst them they were quiet enough, except for the usual witch noises like muttering, cackling and wicked screaming. But in the next moment there was scratching and scrambling and shouting, for at sight of Nightshade the cats put out their claws, puffed up their fur and shot off into the shadows to climb trees. The owls took off in a whirl of angry feathers.

The Head Witch came furiously down at Mrs Rose and Nightshade. "What do you think you are up to, Witch Rose? Really, my dear, a witch can be wicked—but never, never stupid! Why are you bringing a daylight animal like a dog to our festivities?"

"Well," said Mrs Rose, "the fact is, cats make me sneeze. I like cats, but they make me sneeze terribly." The Head Witch was silent with amazement. Mrs Rose went on quickly, "I'm sure Nightshade will make a splendid witch dog. There's a lot to him, Head Witch, and once the cats get used to him. . . ."

The Head Witch was frowning and about to interrupt, when a surprising and terrible thing happened, and took her attention away from Mrs Rose. A large toad, as big as a cat, hopped, croaking furiously, into the circle of witches. Their squeaking, squealing and cackling stopped and they stared most long and hard at the toad. Even Mrs Rose, without any practice, could see that it was no ordinary hop-toad, but an enchanted witch.

"Goodness gracious, it's Smudge—Witch Smudge!" cried the Head Witch. "I must see what's wrong. I'll deal with your problem later, Witch Rose, but I'm afraid it won't do." She turned to the toad. "Smudge, what are you doing here in that condition? You can speak freely. You are among friends. Or is it a joke?"

135

The toad croaked indignantly.

"What?" said the Head Witch. "Not really! Smudge, you *are* a fool!"

She turned and spoke to the other witches. "Witch Smudge has behaved imprudently and has been enchanted by an enchanter for a month. I must say he must be one of the old-fashioned sort of enchanters to turn her into a toad —but he certainly made a good job of it and there's nothing we can do about it. I only wish he'd turned her into a pound of sausages. She deserves it."

A great groaning and moaning and howling burst forth from the leathery throats of the witches and rose up to the moon.

"The fact is," the Head Witch murmured to Mrs Rose, "Witch Smudge is one of the gayest, wickedest witches in our group. She plays the gayest, wickedest witch music. It's a delight to dance our circles to her tunes. . . . And now, she's got herself turned into a toad, the selfish creature. We've no other musician. I don't see what we are going to do."

Upon hearing this, Mrs Rose's silvery dog, Nightshade, sat back on his hind legs and from under his long silvery coat he whipped out a little violin—a little violin made of silvery wood with three green strings and one golden one. He snatched a twig of golden rod, and drew it over the strings, which played a few notes of the maddest, gayest, wickedest witch-music that you ever heard.

The cats slid down from their trees and the owls came circling down out of the night. The witches began to jig and kick, showing their red-and-black-striped stockings. Then Nightshade really began to play, and oh, how those witches whirled and swirled. The owls spun and spiralled in the night air, the cats crouched and pouched and boxed each

136

other with delight in the shadows, while the music grew fiercer and faster and more piercing. When at last it stopped, all the witches, owls and cats fell in a heap on the top of Miller's Hill, legs kicking out in all directions. The

Head Witch disentangled herself, biting somebody's leg as she did so, and felt around among the cats and owls and the other witches until she found Mrs Rose, who was in the dance with the best of them. They shook hands warmly.

"That was no ordinary music," said the Head Witch. "And you are no ordinary witch, Witch Rose. You can keep your dog, and we'll give him the title of Witch-Cat Extraordinary."

So that is why, whenever the witches meet on Miller's Hill for their wicked frolics, Mrs Rose is always dancing among them—one of the most respected witches to come out of night school. And, playing the wild, shrill music on his fiddle, Nightshade dances too—the first dog ever to become a witch cat.

The Kings
of the Broom Cupboard

A family had once moved into a different house. It was just a small family—a mother, a father and a little girl called Sarah. Well, this house was not exactly new—in fact it was one of those big old houses full of space and echoes. Footsteps sounded loud and doors shut like guns going off. The family were all a bit nervous of this different house, and felt it was always watching them, waiting to surprise them. Some of the furniture was inside and some was still coming along in the van, but the inside furniture looked nervous too, probably afraid that its people would go and leave it with no one to dust it or sweep beneath it.

The mother was making lunch when Sarah came and said, "Mummy, you know that big cupboard in the hall?"

"Yes," said the mother, "that's a broom cupboard."

"Well, there's a king in it, Mummy. He's been shut in there for years and years."

"That's a pity," said the mother. "Why doesn't he come out?"

"He can't!" said Sarah. "He's enchanted. Spiders have spun all over him, Mummy."

"Poor king!" said the mother.

"Poor king!" repeated Sarah. Then she thought for a while and said, "Why don't you rescue him, Mummy?"

"I promise I would if I knew how to do it," the mother replied.

"I'll go and ask how," said Sarah and off she went.

Her mother made some sandwiches and cut some cake before Sarah came back.

"You've just got to unlock the door and the king and his friends will come out," she told her mother.

"What? Is it locked?" asked her mother, surprised. "Then how do you know there's a king in there?"

"I heard him whispering to be let out," Sarah said. "There's a draught under the broom cupboard door and that king's got a sore throat. He's had it for years. He can only whisper and rustle. I tried to look through the key-hole, but it was too dark to see anything."

"All joking aside," said the mother, who did not believe in the king for one whispering, rustling moment, "I wonder if we have the key for that door." She took up a key ring from the bench and started looking at the keys.

"This is for the back door, this is for the front door, this is for the study at the end of the hall."

"A witch enchanted the king," Sarah told her mother. "The king and his friends were just having a picnic when, bang, for no reason at all, this witch enchanted them. Then she built a cupboard round them. Then she built a house round the cupboard—this house. That's how it got there. And then that witch just stood there, laughing in a nasty way. Have you found the key?"

"No, there doesn't seem to be any key here," said the mother. Sarah looked worried.

"There should be!" she cried. "The king says today is the day he is to come out."

"He'll have to wait until I find the key," said the mother.

But at that moment a blue pigeon flew into the room. It settled on the table and dropped a tiny black key onto the mother's bread-and-butter plate. Then it cooed in a conceited fashion and did a conceited dance, before it flew out of the window again.

"I told you!" Sarah cried. "It's all working out. That's the key!"

"Well, what a thing to happen!" said the mother. "I wonder if it is the key to the broom cupboard," and she went into the hall to find out. Sarah ran with her.

As her mother jiggled the key in the lock, Sarah called encouragingly, "Are you there, King? Are you listening? It won't be a moment now."

"I'm afraid the keyhole has rusted up," said the mother sadly. "The king will have to wait."

But at that very moment there came a small clinking

and clanking, and four mice came down the hall dragging an oil can. They dropped it at Sarah's feet and ran back to their holes.

"That's useful," said the mother, though she was frowning a bit at the thought of mice in the house. She picked up the oil can and oiled, first the key and then the keyhole.

The key turned easily.

Out from the cupboard came a light like sunshine, the smell of flowers and tomato sandwiches and the sound of drums and trumpets. Out came not one, but seven kings in purple and gold. Out came a whole procession of dancing people in green dresses with flowers in their hair, out came a whole herd of silver deer, strutting white peacocks and a pink elephant with a rose tied to its tail.

Last of all came a witch, dragging a broom after her.

She looked at Sarah and her mother crossly.

"I enchanted myself into that broom cupboard by accident," she muttered. "A wrong word in the wrong place. . . ."

The kings and the queens, the green people, the
silver deer, the white peacocks and the pink elephant
went down the hall in a sort of parade and a sort of
dance. They went one step grave and one step gay, out
into the lovely summer day, off through the overgrown
garden and then into the trees. Their colours shone,
flashed and were lost.

The witch threw the broom back into the cupboard.

"Get in there where you belong!" she snarled. "No
more enchanting for me. I've had a change of heart."
She called to the kings, "Wait for me!" Then she went
scuttling after them like a mud-coloured mouse.

The mother stared after her quite amazed. After a

moment she opened the broom cupboard door and peered uncertainly in.

"There's just that broom left," she said. But the broom went hopping out on its stumpy, bumpy handle, right down the hall, across the garden and into the wood chasing after the witch and the kings.

"Now it's empty," Sarah said with a sigh of satisfaction. "There's room for our own brooms. They should be happy there—it's a nice cupboard. It's good when enchantments work out properly and there's a happy ending."

From somewhere outside came the echoes of trumpets and drums as the kings of the broom cupboard went on their way to wherever they were going.

Aunt Nasty

"Oh dear!" said Mother, one lunch time, after she had read a letter the postman had just left.

"What's the matter?" asked Father. Even Toby and Claire looked up from their boiled eggs.

"Aunt Nasty has written to say she is coming to stay with us," said Mother. "The thought of it makes me worried."

"You must tell her we will be out!" cried Toby. He did not like the sound of Aunt Nasty.

"Or say we have no room," said Father.

"You know I can't do that," said Mother. "Remember Aunt Nasty is a *witch*."

Toby and Claire looked at each other with round eyes. They had forgotten, for a moment, that Aunt Nasty was a witch as well as being an aunt. If they said there was no room in the house Aunt Nasty might be very cross. She might turn them into frogs.

"She is coming on the Viscount tomorrow," said Mother, looking at the letter. "It is hard to read this witch-writing. She writes it with a magpie's feather and all the letters look like broomsticks."

"I see she has written it on mouse skin," said Father.

145

"Isn't she just showing off?" asked Toby. "If she was a real witch she would ride a broomstick here . . . not come on the Viscount."

Claire had to move into Toby's room so that Aunt Nasty would have a bedroom all to herself. She put a vase of flowers in the room, but they were not garden flowers. Aunt Nasty liked flowers of a poisonous kind, like woody nightshade and foxgloves.

"Leave the cobwebs in that corner," said Father. "Remember how cross she was when you swept them down last time. She loves dust and cobwebs. All witches do."

The next afternoon they went to the airport to meet Aunt Nasty. It was easy to see her in the crowd getting off the Viscount. She was one of the old sort of witch, all in black with a pointed hat and a broomstick.

"Hello, Aunt Nasty," said Mother. "How nice to see you again."

"I don't suppose you are really pleased to see me," said Aunt Nasty, "but that doesn't matter. There is a special meeting of witches in the city this week. That is why I had to come. I will be out every night on my broom, and trying to sleep during the day. I hope the children are quiet."

"Why didn't you come on your broom, Aunt Nasty?" asked Toby. "Why did you have to come in the aeroplane?"

"Don't you ever listen to the weather report on the radio?" said Aunt Nasty crossly. "It said there would be fresh winds in the Cook Strait area, increasing to gale force at midday. It isn't much fun riding a broomstick in a fresh wind let me tell you. Even the

146

silly aeroplane bucked around. I began to think they'd put us into a wheelbarrow by mistake. Two people were sick."

"Poor people," said Claire.

"Serve them right!" Aunt Nasty muttered. "People with weak stomachs annoy me."

When they got home Aunt Nasty went straight to her room. She smiled at the sight of the foxgloves and the woody nightshade, but she did not say thank you.

"I will have a cat-nap," she said, stroking the raggy black fur collar she wore. "I hope the bed is not damp or lumpy. I used to enjoy a damp bed when I was a young witch, but I'm getting old now."

Then she shut the door. They heard her put her suitcase against it.

"What a rude aunt!" said Toby.

"She has to be rude, because of being a witch," said Mother. "Now, do be nice quiet children, won't you! Don't make her cross or she might turn you into tadpoles."

The children went out to play, but they were not happy.

"I don't like Aunt Nasty," said Claire.

"I don't like having a witch in the house," said Toby.

The house was very very quiet and strange while Aunt Nasty was there. Everyone spoke in whispery voices and went around on tiptoe. Aunt Nasty stayed in her room most of the time. Once she came out of her room and asked for some toadstools. Toby found some for her under a pine tree at the top of the hill. . .

147

fine red ones with spots, but Aunt Nasty was not pleased with them.

"These are dreadful toadstools," she said. "They look good but they are quite disappointing. The brown, slimy ones are much better. You can't trust a boy to do anything properly these days. But I suppose I will have to make do with them."

That was on Tuesday. Some smoke came out of

the keyhole on Wednesday, and on Thursday Aunt Nasty broke a soup plate. However, they did not see her again until Friday. Then she came out and complained that there was not enough pepper in the soup.

At last it was Sunday. Aunt Nasty had been there a week. Now she was going home again—this time by broomstick. Toby and Claire were very pleased. Mother was pleased too, and yet she looked tired and sad. She went out to take some plants to the woman next door. While she was out Father came in from the garden suddenly.

"Do you know what?" he said to Toby and Claire. "I have just remembered something. It is your mother's birthday today and we have forgotten all about it. That is what comes of having a witch in the house. We must go and buy birthday presents at once."

"But it's Sunday, Daddy!" cried Claire. "All the shops will be shut!"

"What on earth shall we do?" asked Father. "There must be some way of getting a present for her."

"A present!" said a voice. "Who wants a present?" It was Aunt Nasty with her suitcase, a broomstick and a big black cat at her heels.

"Oh, look at the cat!" cried Claire. "I did not know you had a cat, Aunt Nasty."

"He sits round my neck when we ride in the bus or the plane," said Aunt Nasty proudly. "It is his own idea, and it is a good one, because people think he is a fur collar and I do not have to buy a ticket for him. But what is this I hear? Have you really forgotten to get your mother a birthday present?"

"I'm afraid we have!" said Father sadly.

149

"Ha!" said Aunt Nasty fiercely. "Now I never ever forgot my mother's birthday. I always had some little gift for her. Once I gave her the biggest blackest rat you ever saw. It was a fine rat and I would have liked it for my own pet, but nothing was too good for my mother. I let her have it."

"I don't think Mummy would like a rat," said Claire.

"I wasn't going to give her one!" snapped Aunt Nasty. "Tell me, can you children draw?"

"Yes," said Toby and Claire.

"Can you draw a birthday cake, jellies, little cakes, sandwiches, roast chickens, bottles of fizzy lemonade, balloons, crackers, pretty flowers, birds and butterflies . . . and presents too?"

"Yes!" said Toby and Claire.

"Well then, you draw them," said Aunt Nasty, "And I will cook up some magic. Where is the stove? Hmmm! I see it is an electric stove. It is a bit on the clean side, isn't it? An old black stove is of much more use to a witch. Mind you I've got no use for the witch who can't make do with what she can get. I will work something out, you see if I don't."

Claire drew and Toby drew. They covered lots and lots of pages with drawings of cakes and balloons and presents wrapped in pretty paper.

Aunt Nasty came in with a smoking saucepan. "Give me your drawings," she said. "Hurry up, I haven't got all day. Hmmmm! They aren't very good, are they? But they'll have to do. A good witch can manage with a scribble if she has to."

She popped the drawings into the saucepan where

150

they immediately caught fire and burned up to ashes. A thick blue smoke filled the room. No one could see anyone else.

"This smoke tastes like birthday cake," called Claire.

"It tastes like jelly and ice-cream," said Toby. The smoke began to go away up the chimney.

"I smell flowers," said Father.

Then they saw that the whole room was changed.

Everywhere there were leaves and flowers and birds only as big as your little finger-nail. The table was covered with jellies of all colours, and little cakes and sandwiches. There was a trifle and two roasted chickens. There were huge wooden dishes of fruit—even grapes, cherries and pineapples. There was a big silver bowl of fizzy lemonade with rose petals floating in it. All around the table were presents and crackers and balloons—so many of them they would have come up to your knees.

"Aha!" said Aunt Nasty, looking pleased. "I haven't lost my touch with a bit of pretty magic."

Best of all was the birthday cake. It was so big there was no room for it on the table. It stood like a pink and white mountain by the fireplace. The balloons bounced and floated around the room. The tiny birds flew everywhere singing. One of them made a nest as small as a thimble in a vase of flowers.

"What is in this parcel?" asked Claire, pointing to a parcel that moved and rustled. "Is it a rat?"

"It's two pigeons," said Aunt Nasty. "There is a pigeon house for them in one of the other parcels. Well, - I must be off. I've wasted enough time. The saucepan

151

is spoilt by the way, but you won't mind that. It was a nasty cheap one anyhow."

"Won't you stay and wish Mummy a happy birthday?" asked Toby. "She would like to say thank you for her birthday party."

"Certainly not!" said Aunt Nasty. "I never ever say thank you myself. I don't expect anyone to say it to me. I love rudeness, but that is because I am a witch. You are not witches, so make sure you are polite to everybody." She tied her suitcase to her broomstick with string and her cat climbed onto her shoulder.

"Goodbye to you anyway," she said. "I don't like children, but you are better than most. Perhaps I will

see you again or perhaps I won't." She got on her broomstick and flew out of the window, her suitcase bobbing behind her. She was a bit wobbly.

"Well," said Father, "she wasn't so bad after all. It will be strange not having a witch in the house any more."

"Mother will love her birthday," said Claire. "It was good of Aunt Nasty. It is the prettiest party I have ever seen."

"I don't even mind if she visits us again next year," said Toby.

"Look, there is Mummy coming now," said Father. "Let's go and meet her."

They all ran out into the sunshine shouting "Happy Birthday!" Toby had a quick look up in the air for Aunt Nasty. There far above him he saw a tiny little black speck that might have been Aunt Nasty or it might have been a seagull. He was not quite sure. Then he took one of Mother's hands, and Claire took the other, and they pulled her, laughing and happy, up the steps into her birthday room.

154